Dedicated to everyone…

ADAPTATION

This is a work of fiction. Any resemblance to actual events or persons, living or dead, is entirely coincidental.

Edition 1.0

National Library of Australia Cataloguing-in-Publication Entry
Author: Huxley, G. C. author.
Title: Adaptation / G. C. Huxley.
ISBN: 978-0-9923726-0-6 (paperback)
Dewey Number: A823.4

Prefer to read this tale via different media? It has been published in many forms. Your preferred format might be at the author's website:

http://www.huxley.id.au

ADAPTATION

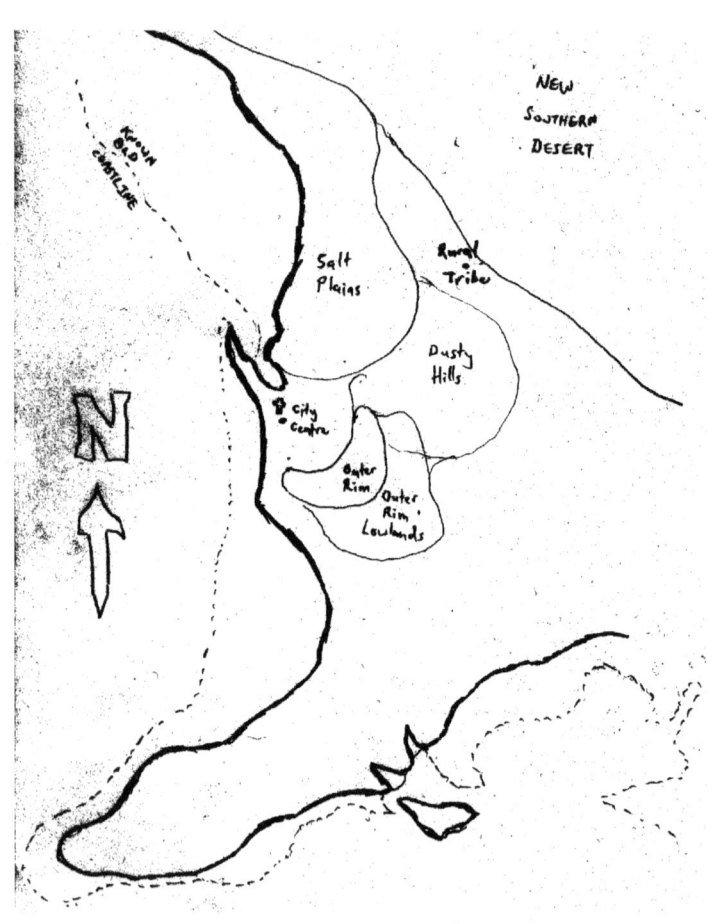

NEW
SOUTHERN
DESERT

Known
Old
Coastline

Salt
Plains

Rural
Tribe

Dusty
Hills

N

City
Centre

Outer
Rim

Outer
Rim
Lowlands

I know this place so well... and yet... it feels foreign, like a dream I had once.

From the hill where I stand, I have a view across the entire valley. Despite little indication of what was there before, everything I gaze at illuminates in my mind unavoidable echoes of past events. Every little re-enacted memory is localised to the region I view, each becoming like a small ghostly theatre.

Even landmarks are like ghosts for me. Where there used to be windmills sprouting from this valley's ridges to provide power to everybody living here, now all I can see are thick shrubs and small trees in their place. I'm confident though that the images of them spinning in my mind pinpoint the exact locations of where they previously stood.

I haven't been back in a very long time, but I just had to come.

What draws us to these places of memory? Whether our stories are good or bad, I think reminiscing is important - maybe? I'm sure that everyone has a place like the one I'm at now.

This place, we called it our 'Sangha'.

I am encountering so many specific recollections, but there is one that stands out above them all for me – something that will always be dear to my heart.

I cannot forget how I came to know the two people most important to me in my life. Way back, in 2073 I think it was, when I was a teenager. A journey enforced by devastating disaster began here, one that gave each of us a better comprehension of the world we lived in.

Maybe it was actually myself I came to better understand?

I wouldn't have known so when I was even younger than that though.

Here in this valley when I was really little, I was bullied by a boy who was staying with us for a while. I know that doesn't make me special, but it had such an effect on me. Garyo Bensen was his name.

I was headed to meet a friend after class, and on this particular occasion the boy had ambushed me by hiding in a tree.

"You're a bastard," he grinned through his teeth, throwing a broken-off stick at me from the branch where he sat.

He was right though, and despite me already knowing it, being told this word to my face hurt. Yes, it was true; I had no father to care for me.

We had been arguing before class started but were interrupted by another excited kid, who had just learnt the true meaning of that terrible word. Most of my recollection is limited to my moment of pain, but I think our original argument was about... whose community wasted the most water? I could never assimilate this boy's mode of thinking. We were quickly diverted though by newly-found knowledge of words of taboo.

Garyo had obviously been thrilled to be able to correctly connect a meaningful insult to something real.

Hoping to escape quickly, I had sprinted along the path, as the jeering taunts echoed behind me. "No dad! No dad! No dad! Why would somebody want someone like you?"

I cried.

I endured so much prolonged pain over this event but, one day, long after Garyo had left the valley, I realised that I no longer felt it anymore. As I had grown, I had moved on.

But that was due to my own experiences, I guess. For when disaster struck my community, it taught me a lot. I discovered others who had met with losses that would have crushed me, having fallen so far that resurrection would be all the more painful.

ADAPTATION

by

G. C. Huxley

Part One

-

Staying By Me

"We dreamt of fighting the forces of evil but when we met the real world it all got confused. I try to be a good person, do what my heart feels is right, but then I sometimes find myself doing the opposite...

Many, many years ago we had already mastered how to obtain the sustenance we needed from this Earth. We've continued to evolve our lives, technology and environment since, but to what benefit? I'm losing the ability to cope... where are we going with our efforts?

So then how are we supposed to know what is right? I think... it's what I can feel deep down in my heart, and I continue to hope it is the same for everyone... even if they're as bad as me..."

1. CLASH FOR SURVIVAL

Waking with a start, the loud rattling of the large vehicles they are riding in is all Rudra hears. Disturbing the peace of the dark, he feels that their convoy is likely the only activity occurring in these dusty hills at such an early hour.

Despite their early morning departure, he is initially surprised he has been able to doze off. Through cracked eyelids he spies his younger sister, Kali, rousing too; he assumes they must have been woken by the same jolt of the vehicle. Perspiration covers her forehead, and he wonders if she has been having the same recurring nightmare she always has, especially considering what they are about to do.

In part routine, she flips open her mobile phone to check for some Internet updates but gives up instantly. They are already far out of range of the city's Wi-Fi network.

"Rudra," she calls out to him, disregarding whether he has been attempting to sleep. "We've been on this for ages... how long before we get there already?"

Rudra gives up and flicks open his eyelids, staring sternly at her for the interruption. *A speedy drive from the Outer Rim of the city is hardly two hours. These days... so calm and resolute... and then so painfully random to handle...*

"Can't be long now at all, are you going to be ready?"

"Of course, I'll be way ahead of you even!" she hurls back at him.

I keep getting the feeling that she doesn't even trust me anymore? Her own blood brother! I hope she understands again one day that she can rely on me to keep us going...

She shouldn't be here... not that she was left with another option anyway...

He steals himself back to the present. "Well remember, once started, there are no more chances to change your mind about this."

"We're all hired to do this because there's no other way... the city can't grow some of those foodstuffs, and these people have no right to them."

Rudra recognises the determination she often displays, unlike many teenagers.

"Don't forget what we're about to do," he growls. "I was talking more about this being your first raid on a Rural Tribe farm." He recalls it is not always an easy job; despite the name given to them, these are modern communities and not the tribes of old. *We don't even really know what goes on in these places either...*

He finds, as usual, that she only ponders his warning momentarily. "I've had enough with the training," she declares with a steely look. "If you already do it then so can I."

~

Dawn is breaking to the screams of battle, some from people who will never see another day. This isn't Bodhi's first encounter with City Raiders and, despite being only near sixteen and scared, he stays true to his role; ensuring the supply of Molotov Cocktails to the front barrier. The Raiders are having a tough time due to the barriers around their valley, and the Northeast ridge only leads to desert. As far as Bodhi knows, it is a surprise attack, and he didn't hear about any diplomatic negotiation.

Suddenly the side gates give way and immediately two City Raiders shoot through – a nimble old man backed up by a teenage girl.

Bodhi gapes at the sight of her; clad in black, her pony-tailed shiny, black hair flashes in the yellow-red morning sunrise, as she simultaneously holds off two of their people by swinging a long staff that ends in a curved blade. Her trained body responds like a dance, in moves far more advanced than anyone of Bodhi's untrained Rural Tribe.

She couldn't be much different in age from me, but is so... impressive...

The two facing her, holding baseball bats and ropes, are maintaining their distance. They are jockeying for a position to avoid her jabs and slashes whilst waiting for openings in her moves, to enable them to get near her for even one swing of their weapons. Bodhi initially thought that wielding such a long weapon would make her slow to react, but her fast combinations of holds, swings and thrusts prove dangerously effective.

He is suddenly clipped around the ear from behind and, discovering Ash behind him, he realises the gravity of what he has just seen.

"Let's get our butts up there quick to stop more coming in!" the young man yells to him.

Bodhi does as he is told and follows him in an instant.

Ash reaches the top of one of the barriers before him, and has already thrown a burning cocktail at a Raider below. Bodhi's mind cringes at the person's shrieks as they are engulfed by fire.

Like an inverse Tug o' War against the invaders, Bodhi helps everyone there to force the top of the gates into closing again. The instant the gates are near closed, more large bolts are thrown in.

Turning to look behind him, Bodhi sees that Ash has collected a bow and a set of arrows and has proceeded along the barrier alone. He is standing still. A City Raider now faces Ash, and a nearby grappling hook can be seen hanging onto the edge of the barrier. In one hand the Raider holds something rarely seen, pointed directly at Ash – a handgun.

Bodhi's perception of time suddenly slows as the two young men face off. He feels his heart beating and the ongoing noise of battle seems to quieten. The Raider's angry eyes, staring out from a large spherical black recycled bicycle helmet, are locked onto Ash. Now up close, Bodhi can see that the Raiders wear thick black leather jackets, zipped up to the neck, with dark jeans and heavy boots. Like the girl he'd seen before, the man has a long bladed staff strapped to his back.

Suddenly the Raider is hit by a fast-moving projectile rock that comes from a nearby Rural Tribe member. The gun goes off and narrowly misses Ash.

Ash must have seen his chance. He instantly charges the man and pushes him over the barrier. The man plunges to his likely death.

Bodhi looks outwards from the barrier and sees the remaining nine City Raiders are already in disarray, forced to run back to their vehicles whilst they are pelted with projectile rocks and fiery arrows.

"Yaooooh!" yells Ash as he quickly appears at Bodhi's side. He and Bodhi grab each other's wrists, dragging each other into a hug and happily slapping each other's backs.

"Wow... you were pretty brave charging that guy with the gun."

"Ha! Someone having that was a bit of a surprise, eh? But since this country used to always have good gun control, I didn't really think he would have more than one bullet."

"What in the Dharma would you have done if he did?"

"Nahh."

"Huh," says Bodhi smiling, and shaking his head at the usual Ash bravado. "Well, there must have been only thirteen of them to begin with though... they must have underestimated us."

Thinking of their numbers, Bodhi suddenly spins to look below for the City Raiders who made it into the camp. The old man lies inert on the ground, alone, and probably dead. The rest of their people have the hostile teenage girl surrounded. She appears resigned to surrender, as she has laid down her blade-tipped staff and is sitting cross-legged on the ground.

Like before, despite the distance from him, he becomes transfixed by the sight of her. *How could something so beautiful bring with it such violence?*

~

Although her skin is fairer than some of the others in the camp, it still has the slight tan of an outdoor life. Constantly mindful of this, Charini wears her favourite wide-brimmed straw hat in the late afternoon heat.

Whilst walking with Bodhi's mother, she spots another friendly face heading in the same direction.

"Dohna!" She waves over to the young woman.

"Okay, I'm off to the Sangha meeting then Charini. Take care won't you?" says Bodhi's mum with a kind smile.

"Sure, you take care too Mum!" Charini knows that Bodhi's mother loves it when she calls her this. The large, warm smile she receives in parting confirms this.

"Hi there Charini, what's up?" says Dohna joining her.

"I've run out of stuff to do and I felt like finding out what some of the others are up to before dinner," the teenage girl says as she brushes a lock of auburn hair behind her right ear.

"Mmm. Okay," Dohna says as they walk together. "I'm on dinner duty tonight too."

"Need any help?"

Dohna chuckles. "No, Nima and Anzan are already rostered, which is plenty."

"Okay..." Her fingers rub the small shiny locket of considerable importance that hangs about her neck. "Hey Dohna?"

"What's up?"

"What do you think is gonna happen at the Sangha meeting?" she asks gingerly.

"You mean to say, what's to be done with our recent visitor?"

Charini smiles.

"You know the meetings are for adults only."

Charini puts on her best sullen face.

"You'll find out soon enough I'm sure," Dohna says to her, smiling at the big guilty grin Charini now wears. The young woman turns to follow Bodhi's mum.

Charini waits briefly, and the moment Dohna is out of sight she sprints off. Since they're not allowed in Sangha decision meetings, some kids couldn't help but find a place to spy on the adult goings-on. All the kids knew about the place, so when she arrives on the balcony overlooking the outdoor fire, she is not surprised to find Tylanni and Nima already there. The two other teenage girls are guiltily startled by her arrival, but immediately settle; Nima sighs in relief, and a deathly stare comes from Tylanni. Charini comes to Nima's side as they resume their positions to view the events unfolding below.

Numerous adults have gathered together in clumps, but overall the group below forms a crude circle. Some stand in the warming breeze and some are sitting on the ground. Charini spots Dohna sitting on a log close to the centre. Many separate discussions are occurring but most of them are inaudible from where the girls are hiding. From what Charini can hear, a large proportion of debates are concerning the person who sits in the middle of the circle – the teenage City Raider girl.

Charini sees that the clothes the girl is wearing really are quite different to theirs. A thin black leather jacket, zipped up to her neck, is not something normally come by in Rural Tribes, especially the zip. Neither are black Capris, nor leggings of any kind.

"Apparently she's done nothing to provoke anyone since," Nima quietly whispers to her. The girl doesn't appear to be resisting at all now either. "When she was brought to the circle centre, she was all, like this, to anyone near," and Nima imitates the girl sheering her body away from unfamiliar entities, repeatedly spinning her head to be ready for danger coming from any direction.

Charini sees the girl now holds her gaze to the ground, avoiding the eyes of everyone upon her. She wonders if the girl is frightened of what might happen to her, or if she is extremely confused by her treatment... this is not a place where someone like her would be in chains or imprisoned.

The girl's clothes look odd to her, and for a moment Charini muses upon how the girl perceives their attire. Nobody wears the same clothes here but there is definitely a theme. Many men wear pocketed utility trousers of differing styles, whilst some of the women also wear the same, in the form of shorts or skirts. Khaki or white sleeveless tops might seem quite common; some wearing collared work-shirts over them, although some of the men have no shirts at all in the heat. Most are tanned from working in the outdoors. Of the people who wear hats though, it might be hard to pick a common style.

"Everybody, please!" says Alexis, in a raised voice. The chatter dies down fast. Charini often perceives her to be unusually tall for a 65-year-old woman, who exudes a commanding presence whenever she speaks. However, she feels Alexis to be quite approachable due to her mischievous mannerisms. As one of the so-called Tribe Elders, she is definitely respected by many there.

The silence is only brief.

"If she knows anyone that cares, they'd likely come back for her, which might be trouble," someone calls out.

"But she cannot conceivably make a trip back to the city's Outer Rim alone either," it's the familiar voice of Dohna. Charini notices that a number of people nod in agreement, and realises that they themselves could endanger this girl. Apparently the way to the city is dangerous at night and, from what Charini has heard about it, the girl would never be able to make the distance during the daytime.

"She's just a teenager... what sort of parents would let her take on this sort of role anyway?" comes a concerned voice from the crowd.

The girl has barely looked up at all to each comment, from her left or right, but something finally triggers within her. "My father? How dare you!" she yells at the ground and the audience quietens. Finally looking up at the crowd, she says, "When he was with us, my father was the kind of man who always had the willpower to do what was needed, to protect what was important."

Despite staring temporarily, most people disregard the girl's outburst and proceed to confer on tribe safety or her welfare.

Really, what can we do with someone like her?

She observes someone chatting in Alexis' ear, who then nods back to the person in agreement.

Actually, I think I already know...

Speaking to the girl in the centre, Alexis says aloud, "You have probably realised by now that struggle or escape will get you nowhere. Do you give us your word that no-one will be harmed whilst you are in our home?"

"Does it look like I have a choice?" grumbles the girl.

Charini spots Alexis' husband, Frank, who stands beside her, silently cursing to himself. He then gruffly says in a raised voice, "I can tell what you're doing – we're going to trust her?"

It appears that Alexis ignores him, for she continues by addressing everyone there: "Compassion is important to our way of life, and you've heard her pledge for our safety. We cannot decide what to do and yet a decision must be made. Therefore, we can only invite her to live among us until then. Are there more ideas or does everyone hereto concur?"

The group suddenly erupts into a large ruckus of feverish debate but they fast fall silent, and the portion that agree raise a palm to the air.

"I'm not too sure about this," Frank remarks aloud to Alexis. "I manage to survive most of your experiments, but this... City Raiders are dangerous." He looks at her sternly but her only response is to wink at him with a smile.

Seeing the people give their vote, the girl appears cornered. "What gives you all the right to condemn me?!" is her furious reply. "I don't need your charity!"

Alexis softly replies for everyone. "Some of us here may be called Tribe Elders, but decisions in this camp are made by all of its peers – everyone in our home over the age of eighteen is before you, and welcomes you."

2. I'M WARY

At the North-eastern side of their valley, the hills rise to a ridge, behind which begins a great desert as far as the eye can see. The desert is still in its infancy; no dunes have formed yet, but life is definitely leaving that earth. Orange-red sands cover stretches of rocky hillsides, with rare occurrences of small, strange, brown plants that still manage to survive there. Orange-red earth facing a blue sky. Known as the New Southern Desert, the ridge overlooking it is a favourite place for Bodhi to sit and ponder, away from the everyday bustle of the camp.

He sits on a rock in his fitted white V-neck sleeveless top, with his slightly-tanned arms resting over the knees of his pocketed utility trousers. He knows that normally he'd likely be staring out across the desert's expanse, but today he can't help but survey what he calls home. Once again the Rural Tribe camp has survived, and for that Bodhi feels glad.

These gifts from the sun, water and the land...

From the ridge he can see most of their valley, which is abundant with numerous different neatly-arranged crops using drip irrigation. He feels the ample amount of food it delivers throughout the year is a bountiful gift, considering that their population is just under forty people. In this slow audit of home it's easy to spot the buildings, the barriers, the small power-generating windmills, and it's hard for him to miss the very tall directed pole that receives the Internet from a distant supplier.

For every centimetre of this valley, Bodhi has a memory.

Bodhi's mum gave birth to him here, and he believes it to be the best place in the world. He feels his mum is kindly enough, and he doesn't consider either of them to be anything particularly special. Actually, he does feel his lanky teenage frame is a bit thin, although his mum always says "You'll fill out, soon enough."

Bodhi wonders again at the attack earlier in the day. He doesn't know what they'd do without the protection offered by the barriers they've erected between the ridges of the valley.

These desperate people, City Raiders... trying to support an ailing city life.

He has only ever travelled to camps similar to theirs and has never seen anything like the city or how the people there live, except for pictures he's seen on the Internet.

Strange towering black monoliths falling into the sea. Twisted metal and concrete.

He isn't confident he entirely comprehends what is in all the pictures. He hasn't even ever seen the sea. One day, if he travels, maybe.

For now though, being in a Rural Tribe is everything to Bodhi. Not just for himself either.

They're such a threat... but... is there another way?
...for my mother too...
I love my home and its way of life, and I WILL protect it... but...
If only something could be done... for everyone?
I guess it doesn't really amount to much though... It's not like a small group like us can affect much...

~

It is time for dinner and Bodhi treks down from the ridge to the evening fire to find people reclining on the Sangha's woven mats and felled logs.

The City Raider girl clearly stands out. She is the farthest from the fire, by herself, and wearing clothing of an entirely different style.

This is the first time he is able to properly observe her, after the demands of this morning's raid. Her black hair is in a ponytail but the strands near her fringe are long, almost touching her neck. She is lying back with her slender legs stretched out and crossed, propped up by her elbows. He assumes the black leggings she is sporting are to give her flexibility for her fighting style. Bodhi feels someone might consider her poise to be elegant and, except for her trained physique, wouldn't consider that this young girl might harbour such fighting skills.

Unlike those engaged in conversation, or staring at the fire or the stars, she is staring into the distance with a face that leans to dreaming of distant thoughts – but tired.

I wonder if she has any family, or anyone?
Is that what she's thinking about?
I'm not surprised all are avoiding her... is it really safe with her here?
City Raider... so she's probably from the Outer Rim... I guess...
Where has she been before? Has she always needed to fight?
Not that I really have any idea what it's like there...

His gaze is interrupted by Dohna coming to the flickering light of the fire. She is starting to serve dinner and carries two plates of food. She walks over to Ash, who is there chatting to a friend, but he stops to thank her for one of the plates and gives her a kiss.

Amongst the happiness surrounding the fire, Bodhi feels odd that the unknown girl is singled out and alone. Normally he might have felt shy about approaching a girl, but Bodhi always has a strong want for social inclusion, so it is partly automatic.

21

At least that is what he tells himself. He isn't quite sure what possesses him to talk to a hostile City Raider, and he now recognises his nervousness. He can tell some people there have observed him heading towards her, and he tries to block out the ideas of what they might be thinking – "Bodhi's gonna to chat up that girl" or "Playing host to a City Raider?"

I'm glad Mum doesn't seem to be here yet... I'd cringe if she stepped in too!

As he approaches, the girl is looking Bodhi in the eye with an unwavering, wary stare and so he gives her a half-smile back. He sits down not far from her and they both look towards the fire.

"Uhh... Hi... My name's Bodhi, what's yours?"

"Kali." She didn't turn to look his way either.

He thinks for a moment to ask how she is, but remembers the day's events and isn't confident about bringing up what is likely a very touchy topic. "Umm... and also that 26-year-old guy over there is Ash... His proper name is Ashoka."

Dohna now approaches Kali and Bodhi with two new plates.

"...and this is Dohna, Ash's girlfriend."

Dohna smiles as she hands over the food to Bodhi, but that melts to a blank face as she passes the other plate to Kali.

Kali eyes the plate's contents as she accepts it but, in neglect, lets the fork slide off the plate onto the ground. Bodhi starts moving to pick it up.

"I can get it!" she snaps haughtily, looking at him as she reaches down. "Eeeyah!" she squeals. In not paying attention, she has to juggle her plate to avoid the food falling off.

Regaining her composure, piece by piece, she faces back towards the fire to begin her meal. Bodhi can see that she is holding herself aloof, likely to be dignity covering up for a clumsy act, and decides to say nothing about it.

"You know, I've seen you secretly staring at me all day. I hope this approach is working out as you'd planned," she says as she eats.

He has already been struggling to develop some conversation but now he really doesn't know what to say. Nothing is spoken as they consume their meals.

Well, I guess I saw her now and then today... but "staring"? Darn it... what does she think I was thinking?

You'd hope she would have been pleased for some friendly words though... considering how everyone here considers her to be hostile.

"Actually, this food grown out here is pretty good, even," she says, sounding enthused, eventually breaking the silence.

"Ah. Good. Freshly picked food tastes great, doesn't it–?"

Kali forcefully interrupts his line of conversation: "Do you want something from me?" She is definitely looking in his direction this time and looks like she expects a response.

Bodhi feels surprised and again, momentarily, has nothing. But then he remembers what also had kindled his interest. "Ah... You showed some quite impressive moves today."

"Yeah, you interested in that kinda stuff too?" she challenges as she puts down her finished plate. "You want a quick spar with me?" She has already stood up with expectation.

Maybe she misunderstood what I meant? Bodhi isn't exactly a fighter and, in fact, has never trained for anything like it yet. She is still waiting though and not wanting to disappoint her, he gets up and stands facing her in what he thinks will look good as a side-stance.

This is the first time they have properly looked at each other eye-to-eye. Bodhi can see that the short parts of her fringe are cut off just before her eyes, which he can't quite determine the colour of behind the reflection from the fire.

Such focused looks on such a cute face, and with the fire dancing in those eyes...

All of a sudden though, he senses a quick burst of movement in Kali. In his surprise to see the world spin, all he can do is spit out "Erk!" He is no longer staring into her eyes – he is now staring up at the stars. With an effortless sweeping side-kick she has brought his legs out from under him. The first thing that emerges from his bewilderment is:

That didn't make me look too good.

...which can easily be summarised by him hearing Kali's "U-huh", as she walks off.

~

Long, brushed, auburn hair flows across her pillow in neat waves.

It is late, and Charini can't help but lie awake in one of the girls' dorms. She replays in her mind Bodhi talking to Kali. Charini knows most of the people in the Sangha and how things generally operate, *but...* the situation of this new girl, this girl of questionable character... it makes her feel uneasy.

Bodhi. He should be more cautious... I mean, I'm only a bit younger than him and we've looked out for each other all our lives... right?

Her mind wanders to an old, happy memory. They were quite a bit younger, doing Sangha chores together; shelling almond kernels. He'd occasionally been flipping almond shells at her hair whilst they chatted and so, feigning a casual walk past Bodhi, she had emptied a whole bucket of them over him as they both cackled.

She smiles happily in the afterglow of the memories. But then, as she turns her head and notices her straw hat discarded on the floor, she feels an uncomfortable strain on her heart.

Her thoughts are interrupted and she looks up to see Dohna visiting the dorm. Dohna gives her a smile, clearly being quiet so as not to wake some of the girls, who are sleeping.

Then Dohna turns around, and ushers in Kali.

She's going to be staying in... here?

Charini eyes her with disdain.

3. SURVIVAL OF IDEALS

Charini sits in the cool morning air with three other teenagers and a Tribe Elder under a very large old eucalyptus tree, waiting for class to start. If it is possible, classes are often held outside. The 'young teenager' ones are always overseen by an Elder, like Alexis, who currently seems to be embroiled in an old book rather than listening to their teenage chatter. She pays no attention to them being seated in their usual spots too; Nima, then Tylanni to her right, with Bodhi behind them closer to the tree. Anzan, another regular class member, is yet to arrive.

"Ooh, I didn't sleep much last night," Charini says, sitting on the grass in her khaki shorts and white sleeveless top, stretching each of her tired legs in turn.

"If it's beauty sleep, I think you'll be needing longer than the normal person, Charini," teases Tylanni.

Nima exclaims tunefully on hearing the taunt: "Ooooooh!"

So horrible. Charini feels that they are always bullying her, and pretends that the comment doesn't mean anything to her. She doesn't feel Nima is as bad as Tylanni though, because Nima can be timid and is usually just a follower.

In hope, she switches to someone she often relies on, turning to Bodhi behind her instead.

"Bodhes. Y'know, this City Raider girl..."

She sees Bodhi raise an eyebrow.

"Her being in the Sangha is no good. She's only going to bring trouble."

"Hah," scoffs Bodhi, who then pauses briefly, like he is mulling over what to say. "Well, uh... your often-friendly attitude... means you are well-liked in the tribe..."

Charini can't help but give a beautiful smile.

"But... you know... you being a stickler for camp rules can sure make you suspicious of someone like her..."

The other two girls giggle and Charini sullenly ignores them. "I bet even your mum told you to be wary of her this morning."

"Well... that probably sounds like something she might have said today," Bodhi says as he obviously pretends to ponder, which makes Charini smirk. "But we've still got to give people a fair—"

With an obvious air that she is busting to enter the conversation, Tylanni interrupts him. "Nima and I saw her this morning! She was doing some sort of training to maintain her psycho City Raider skills."

Nima nods. "She looks pretty dangerous."

"See?" says Charini to Bodhi.

She finds he isn't giving her his entire attention though. "Humph," is his only eventual response.

"Bodhi seems to have taken a shine to the new girl. He's so defensive of her already," coos Tylanni.

"What?" exclaims Bodhi. "No I'm not," he says indignantly. Charini eyes him suspiciously.

Anzan finally arrives. He's a quiet boy and, whilst appearing nervous, sits himself down with the others unannounced. Sensing his arrival, Charini half-closes her eyes and pretends that she doesn't notice. With the way he often discreetly peeks at Charini, Nima has confided in her that she is quite confident that he thinks pretty highly of her.

"Whatever that girl ends up planning, she'll keep it a tightly-guarded secret," Charini announces. Hearing the silence of the others, she spins to face behind her.

Bodhi isn't quite sure if his discomfort is for one girl or the other.

He notices that Charini has now turned back to face the ground where she sits, looking like she's shut the world out for a moment.

Looming near her, and set in quite a contemptuous display, is the City Raider girl. She now wears clothes she must have been given, the kind made by local Rural Tribes; a tough, pocketed khaki skirt and black sleeveless top. However, despite the impending afternoon heat, she still wears her black leggings and her thin leather jacket, mostly unzipped.

Standing beside the girl is a grinning Ash, who has brought her along to the class.

"Right everyone," says Alexis, after being roused by the fuming break in chatter. "As you can see, we have a new person. Her name is Kali and she's going to be staying with us, for a while at least." Her voice changes to a slightly sterner tone. "So, I'd like you all to do your best in making her feel extremely welcome."

Bodhi feels Alexis' gaze as she eyes each teenager in turn. *She mustn't have been so absorbed in that book after all.*

After briefly pausing in thought, a smile starts to rise from Alexis. "Charini... Bodhi... thenceforth it will be your responsibility to make sure that she becomes accustomed here."

Bodhi is never really quite sure where Alexis gets her ideas from sometimes and doesn't really agree that Charini is best assigned to Kali right now.

However... Bodhi conjures a quick vision of a Kali being girlishly happy whilst he shows her about the camp.

27

Not that I can really see her going along with it...

"Great, being babysat at breakfast by him," says Kali, indicating Ash, "and now by two kids."

Ignoring her, Ash remarks jovially to Bodhi, "Ha Bodhi-man, you're gonna be pretty lucky to have two gorgeous girls in tow."

Bodhi becomes quite embarrassed. *Ah, I'm still a bit hopeless with this stuff yet and have nothing to say back... uh... and now the moment's passed.* He hopes he isn't turning too red.

That is until he notices Charini. He knows her too well. It seems almost that a kind word from Ash has dropped her into a blushing dream. He can almost imagine her thoughts right now. *"A compliment from a mature guy like Ash? He's so good-looking too..."*

However, as she spots Kali again and then peeks at Alexis, Charini issues a disgruntled sigh.

Kali has already begun a slow stride to the back of the group whilst all the teenagers' heads turn, watching, with uncertainty. As she slowly takes her place amongst them, she smiles sweetly to Bodhi as she sits down near him.

Her expression changes in an instant.

"Lay a finger on me and I'll break your arm," she says aloud to him, for all to hear.

Yeah right, like I would...

Ash surveys the flustered teenagers and laughs. "Hey, looks like my work here is done then," he says, and he walks off with a big grin on his face. Tylanni and Nima glance at each other and giggle again.

Bodhi can't help but note Kali's abrasiveness. *How is this girl such a grump? I don't think it's actually because of us being a Rural Tribe... Is it me, or does she push everyone away? Like... I don't think Charini takes everything as hard?*

When he looks back towards the front of the group, for a moment he sees Charini looking to the side, with an odd expression, almost dispirited? As she looks up and spots him, she responds with a brief smile, but he recognises the grin as a weak one from her. *Hm... I might ask her afterwards what's going on...*

"Seeing that Kali has joined us, it appears to be a good time to remind ourselves of what is important to our Rural Tribe," Alexis is saying enthusiastically. The regular students groan at the thought.

Kali doesn't seem particularly interested either, but Alexis briefly recounts their way of living regardless; attempting to live sustainably in tune with the environment, whilst being compassionate and conscious of their personal and others' mental and physical well-being. Although they try to use renewable forms of energy, Alexis mentions that they do have a small coal mine too.

Despite her apparent disinterest, Kali wakes up for a question. "Wait a moment, none of this explains what this 'Sangha' thing is you people keep on about."

"Sangha?" says Alexis with a smile. "In some languages the term refers to a place where people have given up previous ways for a better life."

Kali gives an indifferent shrug and glumly faces away again, resting her chin on her upturned palm.

They soon move on to talking about the personal studies each student has been pursuing in their own time. Kali has not been privy to any of it before and, each time Bodhi peeks at her, he finds she is staring off into the distance or twirling a pencil in her hair.

Alexis eventually reaches the next stage in class. "So today's original lecture topic, which delves into more of what we started with, is work. And how do we do work here, Nima?"

After the length of lecturing and reviews, Nima is jerked into inclusion and drones what has been said many times before. "Um, we do our fair share towards everyone's basic needs..."

"Yes! Sharing is one of the reasons for society in the first place."

Bodhi observes Kali rolling her eyes at this statement. Alexis must have noticed too, because she pounces on her. "Don't you think so Kali?"

Possibly due to sensing that she is an outsider to the views of this group, Kali says in a slightly unsure voice, "I... can get by."

Alexis leans close to Kali, her eyes gleaming. "Kali, even the loneliest and most solitary in the universe... the very cold space dust... will eventually come together to form a star."

"Huh, whatever," says Kali, with her face averted from Alexis' gaze. She has had her head leaning on the palm of one hand, and now slowly slides her face down her palm until her fingers touch her forehead.

"If we share the work out according to our needs then we all thereby work less, much less... only a number of hours a day, or more for what we enjoy. However, if we sold our work, we'd all have to work more."

Charini has been studiously giving her attention the whole lesson, but now she is looking confused. However, Alexis is on a roll.

"To explain it better, here's something interesting from history. A hundred years ago, it was normal life that women looked after the house and children, whilst the men would be the only ones allowed to work in any other form."

"Eh?" murmurs Tylanni.

Bodhi finds some of the girls turn to look at him with confused faces.

"What? How is that my fault?"

Nima looks like she is finding it tough to hold back her usual giggles and then he hears Charini burst out laughing. He does notice though that Anzan remains sitting quietly, now with his head held low.

Alexis continues. "For example, everyone here knows that Anzan can be quite a good cook for us in our shared home."

Anzan stills as he is singled out, not wanting the attention.

"But back then it would have been considered women's work, and he would have felt ashamed of it."

Anzan looks like he's entered a remorseful depression, maybe due to finding out that he might be considered shameful in past history. However, Bodhi knows full well the delicious food he can produce and no-one dares to jibe Anzan about it.

"Anyway, understanding led history to make things equal between us. Women were accepted in the workplace meaning that a couple had two incomes instead of one."

"Oh good. So, eventually, all ended well then," concludes Charini.

"Actually, not entirely," says Alexis waving her index finger in a grandiose manner. Bodhi spots Tylanni surreptitiously poking her tongue out at Charini.

"Due to money still being the goal, instead of sharing work, within forty years the cost of living changed to expect two incomes. Despite freedom to work, having more people in the workforce didn't significantly improve life for people at all."

Bodhi looks over at Kali, who no longer leans her head on her hand and is now sitting up a bit more. *Maybe she had started paying attention after all?*

He is caught out by the corner of Kali's eye and he feels her stern glance bore into him as she raises an eyebrow.

He tunes in to Alexis as the Elder's voice is directed to him. "What else do you consider was a result... Bodhi?"

Kali holds her stare as everyone else also turns on him.

"Uh... I guess... even less time for people to support life... like they previously did with a dedicated person at home?"

Alexis smiles. "So, what do we do? We share our work. Without money, thereby efforts can be made that benefit all, regardless of whether they produce something that can be sold... many good things don't."

Alexis surveys everyone at that instant, appearing like she feels she has made her point.

"Right everyone," she asserts, a statement the regular students recognise, making them restless to get going. "It seems like a good point to break. Thanks."

"Thanks Alexis," chime the teenagers in unison, although they have already started preparing to leave.

"Ahhh." Kali exhales as she stretches her arms, whilst the others are loitering about or walking off. Still seated and with her legs crossed, Kali lays her back to the ground. "Well that sucked."

Clutching her school gear, Charini acts like she hears nothing and turns to him instead. "Hey Bodhes, I've got to help out Dohna for a short while. You'll be alright with..." Her speech trails off at the end.

"With what?"

She nods at Kali, who has lagged behind the others and is glaring back at them.

Not that she has anywhere in particular to go anyway.

"Sure," he says in a warm-hearted voice. He receives a thankyou from Charini via a smile, and she disappears in a hurry, probably to get to her chores.

"C'mon Kali, I'll show you around," says Bodhi, smiling to her as she gets up.

She looks him in the eyes momentarily, but then turns. Walking off, with her back still to him, she says casually, "Ah... nah, I'll do my own thing."

~

Charini notes that it is nearing the end of the day; the kitchen's oven light has gone dim, which only happens during the switch to conserving solar power, despite the extra electricity generated by the water moving through the building's pipes.

She has just finished helping Dohna prepare a large amount of seasoned vegetables for the night's dinner. Dohna thanks her, despite it being a routine task, and Charini takes off her apron before walking outside into the coloured shadows of sunset.

She gets that fun feeling again that she often does after working with Dohna.

Ahh, good. All done... love cooking!

Hmmm, food's great, and it's even better when it's done for others.

I wonder what some of the others are up to.

Considering this, she suddenly comes to the realisation that in her haste to get to chores, she hasn't even considered the fact that she left that City Raider, Kali, alone with Bodhi. Her mind clouds.

At that instant, Charini almost finishes walking around the corner of the kitchen building but then quickly steps back again, hiding behind it. She has seen Kali in the distance, loitering around by herself in the shadows near the corner of the corn fields.

What does Kali think she's up to, huh?

Charini presses her body flat against the side of the building, so that just her head pokes around the corner.

She's peering at parts of the valley's barriers...

Her intuition kicks in, and Charini's attention is drawn to what is also in Kali's vicinity.

Oh, she's not far from one of the weaponry stores too! Maybe... she's been past that already? Oh..

If she hasn't seen me yet, then maybe I should be spying on her? Where IS Bodhi?

Charini isn't one for patience today.

I'm not sure what she's planning but it's probably for the best that she is interrupted — fast — especially considering that I was one of those assigned to keep an eye on her.

Charini steps out of her hiding spot and heads straight towards Kali to interrogate her.

~

Really, what does that have to do with the city?

Bodhi is sitting under a tree, reading part of something entitled 'Tales: from the City Lost to the Sea.'

...I'm assuming it's something to do with many city dwellers being Christian...

Kali's arrival has made him mindful of the city again, and the title of this collection he's found on the Internet piqued his interest.

He looks at the verse he's just read once more:

"Seven devils atop tall twin towers
Watch me sin away my fruitful hours
Knowing my folly, they come for me
Enslaving my soul in my melancholy."

The numbers of city-related topics that are a bit beyond his comprehension are mounting. In fact, he is finding that it is becoming an exasperating read. However, with the dwindling sunlight and Kali loitering about nearby, words are rarely absorbed whilst he observes her peer about the camp.

Just then he sees Charini appear and she is striding over to where Kali is. He knows Charini to be a kind girl, although s h e will lambaste him if she perceives he's been up to something... and right now he recognises that style of walk from her. *I'd better get over there before a storm blows up...*

As he jogs towards them, he sees that Charini is yelling and Kali is shrugging her off. However, by the time he reaches them, there isn't much interrogation going on.

"You lot work against the rules. Like, you don't even own this property!" Kali is yelling.

"Own? City dwellers care more about owning stuff than helping each other," Charini squawks, her arms folded.

"Rubbish. We also have the freedom to do what we want!"

"You keep demanding more, and attack us for it!"

"It was you lot that started it – with all the trouble you people have caused."

Bodhi approaches them with an appeasing "Hey, hey," to little effect.

"What in the Dharma are you talking about? Bodhes–" Charini says as she grabs him by the arm and looks up at him. "Tell her what you feel about the City Raider line of work."

Bodhi attempts an apologetic smile of hello to Kali. Her enquiring expression is unwavering, unfortunately. H e isn't exactly eager to be dragged into this mess. Could there be some way where he doesn't have to choose sides? Some way to understand each other's circumstances? "Um... well... with my home and loved ones being under attack... how would you feel Kali?"

She looks down and to the ground. It appears that Kali is becoming agitated with the whole topic, not that Bodhi quite knows what it is.

"Bodhi, you know that us in the city, like you, can also suffer from hunger?"

With that, she turns tail, flicks some of her long fringe hair back, and walks out on the conversation. Maybe he hasn't worded it as cleverly as he thought.

Charini appears to relax temporarily in seeing the back of her, but he knows what is coming.

"Bodhi, you can be so irresponsible sometimes! We were supposed to be keeping an eye on her, remember?"

"I guess I was keeping an eye on her... watching Kali look around was more interesting than what I had in front of me, so... not that I found she was up to anything."

"Watching her was more..." Charini's voice trails off for a moment, her eyes open wide. By her stunned stare he assumes something is about to hit him, but he's not sure what...

"Bodhi!" She yells. "She... ah? She's a City Raider! Well... Now... she could be anywhere! How are we going to keep an eye on her if you make her run off like this?"

He's not sure if he can remember having seen her like this before. His lack of comprehension eventually seems to get to her, as her jaw drops, and Charini rescinds her iron stare to run after Kali regardless.

Bodhi is left only to ponder the storm that transpired.

Charini?

However, if Kali had done something truly bad then I'd have noticed... I'm not that dumb. Charini's just gone nuts... they're both nuts.

Bodhi sighs and relaxes his shoulders.

I'm supposed to remember that negative emotions are only destructive...

What happened between us all was just a mess... I need to review it all, to recognise it another time for us to do better...

Despite all kind intentions though, Bodhi mostly worries about what Kali said.

"...with all the trouble you people have caused..."

He can't shake the debate in his head, and when he finds Alexis that evening to ask her about it, he is shocked at what he hears.

4. ASSUMPTIONS TREAD SHALLOW WATERS

The sun has long since set and the usual laughter is heard surrounding the fire of the Sangha. Bodhi is mostly sitting by himself; Nima and Charini are chatting nearby but they have since sidelined Bodhi long ago, because he entirely lacked the ability to focus on conversation. They leave him to his own thoughts. As the night continues, the excited light dispelled by the fire slows to the ramping glow of hot coals becoming embers.

What he is actually doing is waiting for Alexis. There have been differing people surrounding her throughout the night but, as the last person leaves for their evening wind-down, she draws out the old book she has been reading and stretches out. This is what he has been waiting for – her to be alone. He leaves Nima and Charini to their own debates.

"Hi Alexis… can I ask you something?" he asks, as he drops down to lay beside her, resting on one forearm.

Her eyes flit from her book for only a moment. "Evening young Bodhi, of course you can."

"Were… were there people here before our Rural Tribe?"

Unlike Bodhi anticipates, she doesn't look surprised at all. Instead she casually lifts a finger for him to wait, and she finishes the part she is reading before closing her book.

"It sounds like you've been talking with Kali."

"Uh... well she said things that I found... a bit confusing... troubling..."

"It's okay Bodhi. It was alright to ask," she says softly. "You must remember though – Kali comes from quite a different way of life than what we're used to, and I'm guessing she's been through some heavy ordeals herself."

"Mmm."

"Moreover, don't make too many assumptions about her. She's not just an outsider but also a City Raider – even with compassion, we need to take care."

"I understand," he says, casting his eyes away to the fire. *What does she think my intentions are?* He feels like he is being lectured, when he was originally supposed to be the inquisitor.

Alexis sighs and sits up in a more engaging position for conversation. "What I'm about to tell you is not something we want to hide, but something that is probably better left unsaid until a person is old enough to comprehend what is important... and you are definitely old enough Bodhi."

Something is held back from us? Bodhi feels a slight anxious sense of impending doom creeping in, as if his understanding of his own life may unravel at anything Alexis might be about to tell him. *She is taking it slowly... does she sense how I am starting to feel?*

"What eventually occurred for people in many towns really wasn't important. A large hiccup in history repeating. Life as it used to be seemed to be lost, and would never be the same. If only we had some time to think why, to think clearly, despite what every person became caught up in. Everything was changing within a small number of years. Things then became even worse... it did slow down climate change though... But..."

Bodhi assumes he has lost Alexis to her own thoughts, but her sigh reveals she is ready to continue.

"They were desperate times and we were young, but we had an idea for a new beginning. Before you were born, a small group of us left the city and found ourselves in this valley. There was a farm running here and we could tell it was good soil. We hoped to share the land with the 'owners' and went to offer our labour.

As I said though, they were desperate times; the owner must have already had many people come to try and take 'his' land from him. Not one of our aims at all. He took one look at us and ordered us to leave. We wanted to reason with him but he had already pulled out his shotgun to prove his insistence. We fled to the cracking echoes of his gun. I can still remember the sound of it, as he chased us away.

Our hearts were pounding and our breathing had become strained. You know this valley very well though Bodhi... it was only a short moment before we realised we were trapped against its sides. There were a few young ones among us too. We were cornered.

Realising this, Frank and a couple others who've since passed, automatically retaliated. In the scrub of the valley's bushland we were able to ambush the furious farmer. I can remember it all clearly and yet it was all so confusing; the scuffle of multiple men to disarm the man; the ear-piercing screams of the rest of us watching."

I already know what she is going to say... it's not something I want to hear about our Rural Tribe!

Alexis pauses. She has long since been staring into the coals of the fire. "The man was somehow shot and died instantly. I can't say that it was purely an accident either – primal emotions had risen amongst many. Farmhands arriving at the scene late, finding us now armed and with the dead owner, fled instantly towards the valley's exits."

But I love this place... why'd it have to start this way? Bodhi's thoughts are jammed, repeating the scene over and over, of people he knows in such a horrendous situation. *I've known Frank my whole life... He can be angry sometimes... Does this mean deep down he's a killer? Who else? How many people that I love and think are good? Have I been lied to my whole life? She...*

She can't even remember how much of it was an accident...

"Thenceforth, we lived in the farm. With our innocence lost we resolved to redeem ourselves by our future endeavours... the idea we already had that became the Sangha."

Redeem ourselves??

When reflecting on a few old adventure stories he'd found on the Internet, Bodhi realises that the good versus bad mentality is more clouded than he once thought. *Good defending against evil... defending against the City Raiders... but we took...*

He feels that a small part of a big dream has died.

I wonder if the utopia Alexis had envisioned is actually how the camp worked out...

~

A person is either an early riser or prefers to wake later. Bodhi's mum usually wakes at dawn, to take in the sunrise with some exercise in the fresh morning air. It is far earlier than Bodhi is prepared for, so they rarely eat breakfast together, and they are used to this arrangement. An early morning is especially unwelcome after last night, since it took ages for sleep to sneak past the turbulence of Bodhi's mind.

As Bodhi emerges into the sun, his busy mind dismisses some of the commonplace goings-on of the Sangha. The sounds of sparking welding equipment can already be heard from the repairs shed, whilst a hammer can be heard from somewhere in the distance. A group of people, who have risen earlier, are also walking towards the fields carrying farm tools. They wish him a good morning, to which he gives his usual smile and wave.

He isn't sure how, but when Bodhi arrives at the outdoor area commonly used for breakfast, he finds Charini and Kali sitting near each other on a large log. However, they aren't exactly alongside each other, and they aren't talking at all either. Looking at them, he can definitely sense the lingering tension in the air.

Dohna appears with two new bowls of fruit and hands one to Kali. Bodhi can see that they briefly smile in the exchange, although Dohna eventually ends up seated on the other side of Charini from her.

Maybe it was Dohna, forcing them to be civilised with each other?

Walking towards the group, and seeing the two side by side, he observes that Charini is only slightly shorter than Kali.

They're both quite good looking, although in quite different ways...

They both also want to fight for what they believe is right... although Kali does quite literally.

Hey! Why am I comparing them... especially with Charini as my yardstick? He is saved from his own confusion by his arrival at the group.

"Morning!" says Bodhi cheerfully to them all.

"Hi Bodhi," greets Dohna, although she appears to be more engrossed with her fruit bowl.

"Hey Bodhes," says Charini in a weak morning voice.

All he receives from Kali is "Mm." Bodhi decides to assume it is because she apparently loves eating the fresh food of the Sangha.

He seats himself between the two girls and hears a relieved sigh from Charini.

"Such happy kids, full of youthful energy, ha!" It is Ash arriving to breakfast.

"Alright Ash, settle before you run out of your own energy," comments Dohna.

"My wise lady of love." Ash bends to kiss her, as Dohna smiles. The teenagers momentarily lean away from the couple.

Then Bodhi spots him. Frank is sauntering past the communal area, having just woken up.

"What is it Bodhes?" asks Charini in a concerned voice.

Frank is no longer where Bodhi gazes, and he tears his eyes away to stare off into space elsewhere. "Ah... nothing really."

The revelations of the night before return to flit through his mind as fast independent clips. He keeps adding different faces he knows to the sketchy events that were described but, when he considers his personal experience of each person, nothing seems to add up. *I'm not in this alone though...*

Bodhi peeks to his left and sees Charini and Dohna chatting, whilst Ash is stretching after sitting down. *I don't think I have the right to tell the story to Charini... and I'm assuming that, being older, Ash and Dohna already know it... but... how do they feel about it?*

He encompasses the city, the City Raiders, and Rural Tribes in his thoughts. Trying to find where the balance lies in right or wrong, in so many actions by so many people of the past, is starting to end up as a zero sum.

Is the world always doomed to repeat its mistakes?

Maybe a zero sum is a place to start for things to get better...

If that's so... then there's still a debt we owe here...

"Kali," he says. She looks up at him when she notes his silence. "Our Rural Tribe ways aren't always perfect... you were right about us taking the land."

Kali initially appears surprised, but a smug look slowly enters her expression. She crosses her arms and then frowns in a sideways glance at him. "Well... you're still a misguided fool anyhow. How can the past be your responsibility?"

"Uhm... A person can't really be patriotic to their team about only the good achievements... you've got to account for wrongdoings too... to keep getting better..."

Redeem ourselves.

"Do you always argue this much when you're apologising?"

He smiles. "Kali, I've just been thinking... uhh... would it be possible... please... if you would teach me some of those... self-defence moves... you know and enjoy?"

She turns and scowls at him.

"...I'd like to better myself, so I can help protect what I think is important," Bodhi says in the nicest up-standing tones he can conjure.

Kali pauses, staring into the near distance at nothing. She has heard those words before.

"...*protect what I think is important...* "

Memories of Kali's father come back to her that she can't shake. He is gone, but his ideals and his familiar voice still live in her. *There is always a significant responsibility for people with power over others.*

"Ha, Bodhi-man, are you beating up on girls again?" Ash can be heard saying.

Kali looks over at the boy who welcomed her earlier. She finds him hard to place, compared to those she knows.

Kali is still frowning and stares him down. "Well I guess there's nothing else to do in this boring place!"

~

Bodhi was not surprised that an agreement from Kali had come with some caveats attached. He had to pay attention and follow her rules, otherwise she was quitting immediately.

"Ki-yah!" was the comment from Ash, with his hands in a karate-chop motion. "Just don't come to settle the score with me afterwards Bodhi," he had said to him, smiling. Kali ignored Ash, as usual.

Charini had seemed annoyed with Bodhi for his apology to Kali, and had scorned him with laughter due to the thought of him being told what to do by her. She soon quietened as they walked off towards the desert ridge together.

"Okay," says Kali, turning to stand in front of him, her hands on her hips. They have ensured they are a decent distance from the edge of the ridge. "I'm not going to be your full-time teacher or whatever, so I'm just gonna go through some basics and that's all."

Wow, this is so cool. She is so cool and looking so awesome right now...

I hope this won't end as poorly as the other night...

"Are you listening? Let's start with some simple blocks against punches. If you end up felled by one blow from an opponent, there's no point in learning any strikes. All you do is use your forearms to knock away incoming blows, like this." She is moving her hands upwards and then outwards, her forearms in a windmill motion.

"Seems simple enough," replies Bodhi.

"Well then, now I'm going to be punching you and you need to block me."

"Eh?"

"I'll be going slow at first until you get it."

She positions herself in a side-stance and waits until Bodhi does the same, attempting to mirror her. A slight breeze is blowing up from the ridge, making Kali's ponytail bounce sideways and her long fringe strands lick her chin. Recognising that Bodhi is ready, she tilts her head to nod, then slowly glides her right fist towards him. Bodhi swings up his left forearm and pushes away her wrist.

"That was pathetic," she says with malice. "You have to knock my punch away – it'll be coming fast in the end!"

Bodhi feels hurt by that comment but holds his teenage head from retorting. *If I push it she may give up on this in an instant, I can feel it...* Instead he just gives her a short nod.

Kali's sneering eyes makes it seem like she is waiting for some kind of verbal retaliation from him but, after looking him in the eyes, her expression turns to one of slight surprise. "Okay then, ah... let's go."

She begins to throw some real punches. They are slow at first and he easily knocks them away.

Right, I'm getting this...

He senses a change in her – she has started to speed up. It is in the instant that he suddenly considers their speed that he loses his concentration. The first two knuckles of her left hand strike his jaw and send him reeling to the ground.

Aargh, crud! This is a little rough on a beginner! What on Earth does she...? He looks at the ground and shakes his head. *This anger is only going to ruin my concentration... I need to... focus.* He picks himself up and stands in front of her again, saying nothing but giving her a nod again.

"Huh," says Kali casually. "And after last night I thought this would be over early."

Bodhi says nothing.

"Do I detect some sense of will there?"

"Ah–"

"Yeah? Well, my dad was stubborn too."

Bodhi still says nothing, holding a poker face.

He sees Kali bite her lower lip. "Practice teaches you concentration and also balance. You were all over the place, so it'll need to improve for our next bit – punches."

Great! The interesting part. It soon becomes apparent that there is a deal more to it than Bodhi thought; like focusing punch power in a small zone, body stance and rotation, opponent target areas and a twisting of the wrist with a tight well-clenched fist.

"Just before impact, you need to exhale too," Kali is saying. "Yelling something is a good way to do this as it stokes your confidence and their surprise."

"Yeah, you mean... something like... kiii-yah, I'm a super martial arts master," Bodhi jokes.

A smile curls at Kali's lips. "Whatever turns your knobs."

Did she just grin?

Bodhi has no time to think about it more as Kali suddenly yells: "Now try to punch me! I'll be blocking. Don't give me any of this rubbish about me being a girl, either." Honestly, he initially thought about it that way but he has forgotten quickly with the displays of her capability. Subsequent reminders that she is a girl are just a killer for his focus in another way.

Bodhi comes at her with a number of punches, which Kali easily dispels. He puts a lot of effort into them, as he knows she wants, and from what he has been told he realises how all over the place he is.

45

"C'mon, you can do better than that ya beginner!" She tries to put him off, but then looks miffed, as she receives nothing back but his mental wall of concentration.

Bodhi throws another punch with his left, giving it all he can muster. Kali knocks it sideways with her right, then quickly grabs his wrist with the same hand. She instantly pulls his arm towards her, and Bodhi lurches in surprise, finding that she has stopped short of striking him in the stomach with her left.

Woah...

With a grin of superiority on her face, she now has her hands back on her hips. "Did you see how some of my blocks were in up or down motions, rather than the side-blocks? You've gotta use the top or base of your hand for blocking punches or kicks."

Kali hardly even waits for Bodhi to register his comprehension before moving in for a slow kick. He smacks her leg down with the base of his hand.

She swaps to the other leg and gives another, this time much faster. He manages to get that too, just in time. They momentarily pause, and Bodhi senses that she is becoming chagrined by his luck.

She is coming at him again, with the movement now seeming to be in slow-motion for Bodhi. He can see her slim trained body begin to twist whilst her black hair swirls, until he spots a look in her eyes that hasn't been there before. Bodhi brings his hand down way too late as her kick comes at his body, and in his current balance he has to dive sideways to the ground to avoid most of the force.

Kali pauses, watching the boy hold his side as he rolls over to face upwards, and then her emotions suddenly come to the fore.

"You fool, you could've been hurt!!" she yells at him, feeling completely flustered.

"It was close, but I'm okay," she hears the boy saying. "You okay?"

For a second, this stills Kali in mid-thought...

"I'm fine!!" she splutters, lowering her head.

It's all too confusing.

This has to stop, now.

She decides to leave the boy there and turns before he can even get up.

"Don't make me do that again!"

Getting to know someone just leads to disaster...

5. STAY WITH ME

I like the way he laughs.
I like his strength in mind.
I like the way he hopes for the best in everyone.
I like him.
I can't have him.

Charini allows her head to drop back into the pillow and stares at the ceiling of the dorm, her memory of yesterday replaying, again; her heart in her throat as she angrily yells at Bodhi, only to have him turn and walk off with Kali; Charini then disappearing before Ash or Dohna can see the tears in her eyes...

But he's my friend...

She now feels even more bewildered. She expects others experience confused heartfelt feelings, but for her there is something else. She instead feels... heavy. An immense well of bitter sadness seems to ask her to weep for herself, but she doesn't quite feel like crying. There is no class this afternoon but there are still chores to be done, but she just can't bring herself to go.

Am I so bottomed-out that I've just run out of tears for myself?
What is wrong with me?

...

Charini holds her fist firmly clenched about the locket at her chest. The locket normally calms her but today this instinct offers her nothing.

What is it? We've spent so many good times in our lives together...
Does it not mean anything to you Bodhi?
We've been such great friends, is that as far as your care for me goes?

An image of Kali flicks into her mind. *Is it her? What could he feel about her?*

She is quite gorgeous though...

...

No one has really told me if I'm actually beautiful. Well, a few of the Elders but... they were probably being nice to me. Nobody that really counts.

Her own versions of the hurtful things that Tylanni often says to her come to her mind;

"...clumsy..."
"...not beautiful..."
"...no parents..."

...

I shouldn't pay attention to her...
What if she's right though, and that's what many people think?

She then finds the echo returning: *"What is wrong with me?"*

Those words bounce around in her head a bit longer, dragging her lower, as she feels it more – that despairing heavy feeling. It is like a secret dull pain that she wants to rip from herself screaming, and yet it seems like she can't move at all. She really doesn't want to get up.

I think I've felt that feeling before... for some time now.
It's like I'm in a pit, peering upwards at the world passing me by.

...

Er, I guess Anzan likes me, I'm pretty sure. But what does he know?

49

There is a knock at the door and it is *him*. Charini cringes in her mind, somehow doing it carefully, in case it shows on her face. *The person I probably least want to be seen by at my worst...*

"Hey Charini! We were about to get started on our chores but you weren't about? I even got Kali there... eventually."

"Ah, sorry. I just wasn't feeling too well for a while, so I took a rest." *Not good at all... please don't interrogate me.*

"Are you feeling okay now?"

"Yeah, just head on and I'll be up in a sec."

"Okay." He turns and heads for the door.

"Bodhi," she calls after him. "Do you trust Kali?" Then quickly: "With her being a City Raider, remember?"

He stops briefly, in thought. "Uh... well she's a little rough around the edges, but... yeah."

"Ah, she has nightmares."

"Hmm?" she hears a questioning Bodhi, the sound of his footsteps stopping.

Why did I mention her nightmares? Some hopeless attempt to bring her down again? Am I actually seeking compassion for her?

I'm all a bit lost...

She looks to Bodhi again to find him waiting – expecting something but not sure what.

Charini stares at the ceiling again briefly, and then sighs. *I'll have to get up.*

~

After Charini is able to finish her share of the chores, she vanishes. Kali and Bodhi are not so fast. It becomes quite late and they have to rush to the meal area together.

"Have we missed dinner?" asks Kali.

"It looks like it," says Bodhi, looking about the Sangha's fire. "Hang here though... I'll find us some of the leftovers."

As he walks back to her, empty handed, he finds that Kali has seated herself on the ground far from the fire and is looking up to the sky. *Is it so that she could see the stars better?*

Hmm... More likely though... it's to sit away from the small groups of other people here...

She brings her head back down as he approaches and he notices the expression on her face.

"My mum was finishing up in the kitchen building... she said she'll sort us something," he explains as he tiredly plonks down next to her. "You did well with the almond harvest... took it in your stride."

"Just whacking trees with a light pole, any simple girl can do it. But, it seems like I have a knack for that style of work somehow."

Bodhi smiles at her joke. He isn't feeling as nervous around her this time, especially after the experience of some tiring work together. It has been quite fun too despite the fact that while watching her work, it looked like she was using it as some kind of training exercise. He realises she appears to have let her guard down slightly too, possibly for the same reasons as him.

"It took longer than normal though... we deserve a good dinner."

She gives him a displeased sigh. "I've gone past the hunger point already anyway."

Kali then motions him nearer with a nod and quietly whispers, "Who's the guy with the drapes on his head?"

Bodhi looks to where Kali's gaze is fixated – a strange man sits by the fire, his back leaning against a log, alone.

"A nomad."

"Like some sorta guy that wanders the desert?"

"It's not really wandering... more like a seasonal migration between known places..."

To Bodhi, this man's appearance is no different to other nomads he's seen in his past. The cloth the man has draped across his head is made from long woven wool of black-and-white stripes, with a length that reaches to his belt. Otherwise his clothes are just like any other person's, but limited to only simple styles. Attached to a strap that comes across his chest is a small leather drinking pouch. Besides this, he seems to have nothing except for a few items strapped to his belt.

Bodhi can't help but stare at him and wonder.

"They tend to keep to themselves... it's pretty rare to see them... Maybe he has come looking for help? In obtaining some medicine?"

Fidgeting, Kali picks up a nearby stick. Bodhi watches as she slowly starts to draw a line in the hard red dirt with it, seemingly in a musing trance.

"Hey Bodhi, you... you know that City Raiders are told to raid for food because the city doesn't have much choice, don't you?"

Such a question from Kali, where's this coming from?

"Er, sure." He doesn't really understand the reasons properly but wants to sound reassuring.

"Um... good." She lifts her face to the sky and closes her eyes, like he gave the right answer.

Bodhi leans back and looks up at the array of stars. "I just wish... there was a way to sort things... so that we could be safe."

She jams the stick into the ground. "That's a bit selfish, really... If just the Rural Tribes survive, and steal the land to do so!"

"I meant so that all people can be safe..."

"Even City Raiders?" asks Kali. It feels like she is testing him.

Should I say it?

She might...

Argh, enough thinking -

"...and you too Kali."

Kali stops drawing in the dirt and she looks up at him like her eyes are searching for something. It seems like eternity has greeted Bodhi. He feels he might get lost in the chance to stare at such beautiful feminine lines of her soft face.

This is all instantly drawn away, when a change in her course of thought can be seen, as her expression switches to a frown. "What makes you think I need your help?"

Oh no. Definitely not what I meant... at all. "I... don't... All I was saying was—"

"Oh, poor Kali," she is saying in a sing-song voice with her face cast downwards again. Bodhi can't see her expression for her black hair hanging down, but when she looks up he sees that her eyes are almost closed, steeling within herself for the building fire inside.

She gives an exasperated grimace as she stands up and bends over him, drawing her face right down to his. "I don't need your help! You got that?"

They are staring each other in the eyes but neither of them is saying anything.

Such an intense look on her face. Bodhi senses that the conversation around the campfire has suddenly gone quiet. His thoughts are quite mixed, and he worries at what expression she sees on his face. However, being in that state and a guy, it probably expresses nothing.

The corners of her mouth turn down as she draws herself back, and then Kali ends the conversation in her usual way — she leaves.

~

"Kali..."

What was that?

She dozes deeper, heavily asleep in the late evening. This dream is different to her usual recurring nightmare though. Something is calling her name.

"Ka-li..."

Is it my brother? Rudra? It is becoming confusing.

The voice seems to growl this time: "...Kali." It might sound like her brother.

Is this real?

...

If I left the camp...

Her mind moves on to thinking about her time at the Sangha so far, ...

Grr, I need to get my head together.

She manages to rouse herself from her dream state. She surveys the girls' dorm and finds them all asleep, including Charini.

~

Charini wakes in surprise, as a group of people of the Sangha bust into her dorm.

"What're you... all doing?" she squeaks. Still only half asleep, she peers through long auburn strands with bleary eyes, blinking in the morning light.

But there is no-one there – disappearing just as quickly as they arrived.

She throws a large khaki cloak around her pyjamas. Rubbing her eyes as she walks out into the morning sun, the first person she encounters is Dohna.

"We found one of the barriers open this morning," says Dohna without greeting.

"What?" exclaims Charini.

"It looks like Kali is gone too. We're currently checking around the camp though, in case something more sinister is going on." Dohna's eyes are looking about, watching the commotion of the searching Sangha members, whilst Charini registers what has happened.

"I guess her departure will let everyone relax a bit again?" Charini says finally.

"Hmm, yeah. Good for some, but not for all," says Dohna, as she points towards Bodhi, who is sitting alone on the desert ridge.

Seeing him brood up there makes Charini feel weird, almost angry. *What an idiot!*

She has to go see him to understand better for herself too, and hikes up there. A chill breeze is blowing from across the desert and up the ridge, making Charini hug her cloak around herself. As she approaches, she sees that Bodhi is sitting on a large flat rock. He gives the impression that he is undisturbed by her imminent arrival, either because he knows her well and is ignoring her, or is deep in thought.

"Bodhi, this was always going to happen," Charini says as she eventually reaches him, like Kali leaving was a sure thing.

He is looking out across the desert and doesn't turn to look at her. "Mmm..."

"She was a City Raider... You know she lives elsewhere." She stays silent momentarily but still gets no response. "I can't believe that you liked her." Charini watches him intently.

Looking down at the ground, Bodhi still doesn't move, but his reply is quick.

"Kali? Her? Nah... Something like that would be crazy..."

At that Charini feels a slight release but no elation at all. *At least he might not be in love with her...*

But she feels no consolation either. "Well... yeah, it'd be pretty dumb..." she mumbles. "I don't know what in the Dharma you think you're doing here then..."

She's heard enough for now and saunters off. *Maybe I've been too hard on Kali?*

Out of the corner of his eye, Bodhi detects Charini leaving and turns slightly to watch her walk away.

"Charini?" he calls out.

No response.

I need to do something to get in focus. Bodhi shakes his head and lifts himself up. Remembering some of the moves Kali taught him yesterday, he practices them all morning until someone finds him for lunch.

6. THE CORE OF SOCIETY

Two nights have passed. It has been quite easy for Charini and Bodhi to return to the regular rhythm of the Sangha, almost like nothing has happened.

"Considering all the problems that Kali caused, it's better this way." The morning class is soon to start, and Charini has previously brought this up with him a few times.

"Yeah... I agree," Bodhi finally says.

He feels glad that he was able to learn some combat moves from Kali before she left and he practises them each day, including early this morning. He hopes he is improving, despite the lack of instruction.

In fact, Bodhi realises he has a bit more confidence with himself overall since Kali left. *Who needs her... anyway?*

Bodhi looks at the group sitting on the grass: *Charini, Tylanni, Nima, Anzan...* His gaze passes over to Alexis quizzically but, still reading that book, she looks in no hurry to start the class.

Bodhi's search is interrupted by Charini, who must have realised his state of confusion. She has put her hand on his knee and is lifting a finger to point behind him. Her brows are furrowed upwards, her mouth agape.

Looking over his shoulder, he finds that Ash is approaching, with Kali in tow.

Again? How?

Ash breaks the silence whilst holding a big grin. "Ha, hey Bodhi, look who's back hey…"

Bodhi's mind sneers at the slight insinuation and sets a glum look on his face. *Ah crud, what if he gives Kali the wrong impression though?*

Kali gives no indication and keeps her head held high, as she moves to take a place amongst the group again. She is still wearing the same clothes, the thin leather jacket and khaki skirt, but her appearance is dishevelled from her short adventure.

"Ash?" quizzes Charini. "What's going on?"

To that Kali sighs in a displeased slow "Huumph."

"We found her outside the barrier. She said she'd tried to cross to the city but had to return due to a lack of supplies."

Bodhi looks to Kali but she is ignoring everyone's inspection. *She seems sad… maybe? I wonder if there is anything that could… make things easier… whilst she's with us?*

"All I told her was that she was just in time for class to start… Ha! You should have heard her groaning, until I said that we still had some breakfast left."

Kali rolls her eyes as the girls chuckle. Bodhi can't help but grin, but notices that Anzan is looking away, like he pretends to hear nothing.

"Well, I'm off," says Ash as he raises his palm to Alexis. She does the same and nods. As he parts from the group, he leans down to nudge Bodhi with his elbow in an insinuating manner. Bodhi's mind clouds, until he catches Charini shaking her head slowly. *Is that for Ash? Me? Probably both of us…*

"Okay everyone," starts Alexis in her commanding voice. "Shall we talk today about… love and suffering?"

Talking about love? In class? In front of the others? Bodhi avoids Alexis' gaze, and notices most of the other teenagers curling up too. Nobody says anything. This topic only leads Bodhi to think of one person, a heartfelt secret which he dare not share casually with the group.

"Bodhi, what about you?"

"Eh??"

"Your mum?"

"What?!"

"You know it boy!"

"Huh–"

"Think quick!"

"Wai–"

"The first thing that pops into your head!"

"Ha, ha, ha!" Charini is giggling out loud near him, the others too. "You've got to give Bodhi some of his musing time... I'm sure that Bodhi's mum wants to be loved, and we all love her very much."

Alexis smiles.

"Yeah," says Bodhi sheepishly, but he breaks his mood with a grin before poking his tongue out at Charini. "What she said."

"And so someone tell me something about suffering then?"

The class becomes quiet again.

Bodhi isn't quite sure what will suffice as an answer. He can think of many things, but feels defensive when considering the others around him.

Lifting his head he finds Kali to be looking about herself at everyone quietly pondering, and she becomes the first to speak up.

"This lot wouldn't know suffering, even if I whacked them one."

"Have you ever felt that you were suffering, Kali?" says Alexis softly.

Kali goes mute, and backs down in an instant.

Alexis continues regardless. "Sometimes it is hard to understand each other. We constantly delve into or try to judge each other's actions. However, in knowing that every person does feel like they're suffering, and all want to be loved, we can all find common ground between each other."

This seems to make sense to Bodhi. *But how far could this really be useful?*

"Could you find... or even would you share... should you share... that sort of common ground, even with someone that does something extremely bad?"

"Think about it, young Bodhi; how they feel, or, the motive for their actions. When you get deep down into every person, it's universal."

~

Charini, Bodhi and Kali sit silently around the crackling evening fire of the Sangha. Nothing is being said at all, although it's easy for Bodhi to assume that everyone's minds are very busy.

He sees Tylanni and Nima wander past and, when they see Kali, their chatting swaps to hushed whispers as they scuttle off.

He receives a nudge from Charini but he doesn't want to. He instead nods back to her that she should ask Kali. She insistently jerks her head in Kali's direction.

Bodhi is about to give up and turn to question Kali, when the loud warning alarms of the Sangha suddenly start clanging.

Trouble!

He sees Charini leap up and sprint in the direction of her emergency post, without saying a departing word or looking behind her. Bodhi rises to do the same, but suddenly Kali calls out to him.

"Bodhi!"

He glances back at her and is surprised to see her desperate face. *The girl that often holds herself so confidently... looks completely rattled...*

"Don't go out there," she begs. "I've..."

"Kali?"

He then turns away from her. *I don't have time for this!*

Bodhi heads as fast as his legs will carry him to the barriers, with Kali in tow. As he sprints he can see others running too, and all are headed in the same general direction, towards the corner of the corn fields at one side of the valley. He hears clanging alarms again and can tell they ring from where the people are headed, and it spurs him on faster.

He knows this side of the valley. There is less of a man-made barrier here as it leads up to a ridge that leads down into a maze of rocky outcrops with crevices, which they have filled with traps instead. For this reason it is also rarely guarded, and only occasionally patrolled for signs of trouble.

Reaching the top of the ridge, panting like the others, he pulls himself up short when he glimpses what is below. Kali too, as she is only seconds behind him.

Bodhi's heart sinks. *City Raiders from the Outer Rim have returned... and this time with double the number of people.*

They are each perched upon different rocks, armed to the hilt, but not moving.

Bodhi bewilderingly looks around. Most people of the Sangha about him are watching below them and saying nothing, as a cool breeze blows up the ridge.

What are the Raiders d...? They seem to be waiting for something?

A period of time passes and Bodhi avoids looking at any of the traps that are blocking the City Raiders. Their assailants are here for a reason, but nothing seems to be occurring.

Then Bodhi hears the voice of a man call out from amongst them, from an indiscernible speaker: "We know that there is a coal mine on this land..." The voice stops and, in the silence all around, the resounding echo of the voice slowly dies out.

The people of the Rural Tribe are all looking to each other, but have yet no response to give.

No demands?

"Leave peacefully now, or we will force you out!"

Nothing else can be heard but the continuing breeze. People on both sides appear to be at the ready for anything, but it seems that nobody is willing to make a move. Whispers abound on both sides of the impasse.

"Kali!"

Apparently recognising the hoarse voice from afar, Kali stiffens, and so Bodhi peers down to the stranger who has called out.

"Have you forgotten?! Whadda ya think you are doing?! Disable these traps NOW!"

Bodhi has disregarded the relevance of Kali up until now. Looking to her again, he finds her surrounded by faces full of accusation. As he studies her, sh e appears to be unable to move, and when their eyes meet she casts her gaze sorrowfully away as she bites her lower lip.

With his mind awoken, he instantly realises where she is standing: only metres from the safety lever that disables the traps.

Bodhi feels a strong force building within, a feeling as if his eyes are bulging, his mind on full alert.

She told them about the coal mine?

Everything was going so well... Didn't she like us? But...

Kali is not moving though.

Everyone was warning me...

Only confusion is stopping him from completely realising his anger. *Was I stupid to think I was learning to trust her? When, or how did she change her mind?*

She still has given no response and the man appears to be furious. "Kali!!" he yells and echoes.

Clearly exasperated and, taking efforts into his own hands, Bodhi sees the man climb down into part of a crevice that contains one of their traps. It has become partially exposed and it is now obvious how to disarm it.

I t is a decoy. A tripwire is sprung and large steel spikes swing from nowhere, piercing the flesh of his chest. He gives out a ripping scream that ends in a gurgle.

"Rudra!!" shrieks Kali in extreme distress, and throws herself towards the master lever.

Bodhi tries to pull her away and, without looking back, she delivers a sharp kick to just below his chest. He is knocked to the ground and can hardly breathe.

Slightly raising himself and reaching forwards, gasping for breath, he grapples for her ankle but he can see it is going to be too late.

Kali feverishly pulls the lever.

As she sprints below for the man, Kali quickly vanishes from Bodhi's view; throngs of people from both sides have launched themselves across the hillside to meet each other in battle.

7. LIFE SUPPORT

Bodhi cannot remember a conflict as devastating as this. Nobody can be considered victorious – all experience defeat.

The battle has killed or wounded the majority of people from both sides, and they have to set up extra tents to care for such a large number.

There will be no sleep for anyone tonight.

It is the next evening and Bodhi sits beside his mum. Her injuries aren't currently life-threatening but she is still bound to her bed with odd bouts of sickness. He is quite confident of her being okay, but worries all the same. For now he is resting himself whilst she sleeps.

Despite being one of the wounded herself, Alexis has asked that all be cared for, regardless of whether they are a City Raider or from a Rural Tribe.

Also among them are Frank, Tylanni and Dohna. Charini has been to see them occasionally but is running around a lot, as others are, tending to such a large influx of the unwell.

You probably haven't seen to that guy named Rudra though, have you?

Charini has told Bodhi that she can hardly fathom her own harsh resentment with what she feels Kali brought upon them all. She said she feels tired – her mind is tired – but her love for the people there is spurring her on.

Bodhi doubts that other able-bodied people of the Rural Tribe are much different. There is such confusion: caring for your persecutors; worrying about the welfare of your loved ones. *How will the Sangha rebuild and function in the future after such an overwhelming battle?*

Despite these thoughts, Bodhi feels that Alexis always has her finger on the pulse of the Sangha. From what he can remember, Alexis has said something like:

"If all who are left are grieving and in disarray after we are gone, I will be also, but if you all work together with strength for the future, then I'll be able to leave in peace."

Some were not happy with her for talking about death, but for others the speech spurred them on – maybe in regards to her words, or just plain respect.

Bodhi tiredly opens his eyes and surveys the weird scene of bustling attendants and doctors. *This is a disaster. Conflicts are our failure... and so often involve the innocent...* For a brief moment he remembers the story from Alexis of their past. He feels sick. He feels sick.

He shuts his mind off for a bit with some breathing exercises he has been taught, and eventually feels a bit more in control.

I have ideas of how this came about... and Kali was primarily involved... but I don't really know the details of it. Is this what she wanted? Was she forced? How do I understand someone like her... or even ask her about it?

Bodhi then isn't sure if he feels angry or that his trust has been broken. He previously felt he was getting to know her but now the divide between them seems even greater. *That girl would probably rip into me if I asked... What was happening before her brother became injured?*

He looks over to where Kali is. She hasn't spoken to Bodhi since, like she is avoiding him.

By the way she holds herself, seated alongside her brother, it suggests to him that she is extremely tired. Her black fringe in the yellow lamplight helps to cast long dark shadows across her still face. Rudra is not moving and her downcast eyes seem fixed on watching her brother's wheezing breathing chest slowly rise and fall.

And then it stops.

"No!" she shrieks. As Kali suddenly rises to stand over Rudra, she knocks everything off his side-table. Nearby Sangha doctors rush over and start to attempt to resuscitate him.

"Noo-hoo-hoo!" she howls as she is pushed aside, her wail almost ending in stuttered crying. Then suddenly in angered tones she yells, "You can't leave me too!"

But there is nothing to be done, as Rudra is the next to be lost.

~

It is all surreal, like a dream of something that hasn't happened – but it has. The shocking hit of one event redirecting lives onto an unknown, and similarly impermanent, new pathway.

Kali weeps uncontrollably. Without really thinking about it, she finds that she has fled to the desert ridge.

Somewhere away from these people...

As she slowly looks up from where she sits, Kali calms slightly as she stares out across the desert. The expanse of that empty void is always greater than anything in her imagination. It is a dark blue in this dead of night, only partially lit by the moon.

Depending on someone is just too dangerous...

She sniffs and stares further out, her eyes welling with more tears.

If I walked out there, it would complete my loneliness...

Bodhi realises that she hasn't yet noticed him; he started looking for her after he saw her run off. Her back is to him and he can hear her occasional sobs as she looks afar.

She's been in a bad place for so long... I want to hold her so much... Although she'd probably break my bones if I tried it...

Instead he shuffles forward to stand beside her and also looks out across the desert.

What can I say? Uhh... er... "As long as humans are social animals with the adversity of change, they will group, and will never need to carry the burden alone."

The smell of pollen blows in from the distant rocky outcrops. Despite the desert's harsh nature, it may not be dead yet.

His words sound to her almost like another camp lecture, but for once she doesn't want to tell him to go away.

EPILOGUE

How long have we been walking for?
This is all happening too fast, like a dream... a nightmare... and I bet it's only going to get worse.
Charini listlessly walks along a dirt track covered in weeds, surrounded by the remnants of an over-logged forest.
She looks ahead and sees Bodhi still there, trudging along too.
Dear Bodhes. I wonder how you feel about everything?
Leading the three of them is Kali, and Charini detects a glint from the long bladed staff strapped to her backpack.
How could I have been so stupid to agree to this?
I really am hopeless...
She stares even closer at the girl.
None of this would've happened; we wouldn't be here now, if not for her...
I still wish we'd never even met.
Even though she offered to help that day... when it was all becoming worse...

~

Kali had been peeking into the tent, making especially sure that nobody saw her. She told herself she was interested because the goings-on there were currently the major focus of the camp.

She had heard from Bodhi that the situation was now more than just tending to wounded victims. At first it had been a lower priority, but as more people succumbed to it, the Sangha doctors had realised the seriousness of it. Despite their healing physical injuries, hospitalised people from the Rural Tribe remained sick, just like Bodhi's mother. It also appeared that the City Raiders were immune to it. The doctors were apparently at a loss – they had no idea what it was, let alone how to treat it.

Eventually Kali opened the tent flaps wide to allow her to enter. It made many people look up, and many continued to stare; they were looking at one of the causes of the unfortunate situation. Kali avoided people's gaze as she strutted to where Bodhi sat with his mother.

Bodhi saw her approaching. He sighed.

"Hi Kali... what's going on?"

"Bodhi. Is your mum getting better soon?"

"Well, her injury has almost healed... but..." Uncontrolled assumptions of future outcomes started appearing in his head again. "This illness..."

"Mmm." Her gaze seemed to avoid his, observing nothing in particular, and she kept twisting on the spot.

"Kali, tell me what's going on?" Bodhi asked tiredly.

"Well," she whispered, looking sideways as she pouted. Bodhi was not feeling entirely patient with her, but then she added, "I think I've seen this before."

Bodhi went wide-eyed, grabbed her wrist, and proceeded to lead her from the tent.

"Hey?" yelled Kali with a cross expression.

Charini approached them. Her eyes met with his like she recognised this kind of serious worry from him.

"Let's go see Ash," he said, and Charini followed them out.

With the state of the Sangha and those who were in good health, it had fallen on Ash to be one of the de-facto decision makers. There wasn't always time anymore for large meetings of peers. His usual jovial manner had been temporarily put aside for fleeting moments when it was appropriate.

Nearby folk had seen the teenagers run to meet him and, after his exclamation and seeing him running his fingers through his blond hair, some came up to hear what the commotion was about.

"You have to believe me!" Kali was saying. "I have seen this before, when I was little. You need to give me enough supplies to get back to the Outer Rim."

"This seems like a ruse," was a gruff comment from an approaching Tribes-person. There were murmurs about trust.

"Don't you understand?" Kali said angrily. "If I can't get this cure then, in the coming months, these people will all be dead!"

Everyone was silent, seemingly unsure of the next move in debate.

Sensing he was getting to know Kali more than the others, Bodhi decided to step in.

Mum...

I must be calm and in control.

"Kali," he began. She spun to face him as he spoke; she looked poised for any rebuke. "Due to recent actions, what people are feeling has a basis..."

"You may well think that, I mean, after my brother died, what is keeping me here anyway?" retorted Kali.

Bodhi felt that her emotions had been like a rocky boat since her brother died. The voice he heard was loaded with both sarcasm and despair.

He paused and then continued. "...and that's why I will go with you."

Kali's first response was to scowl at him, but then she said: "I am going to be the one doing this!"

Bodhi, however, elected to give no response.

Kali broke off her stare and folded her arms. "So much gratitude in this place!"

I must do something for Mum... if what Kali says is true...

Can I trust her?

...

I have no choice...

Up until now, Charini had been quietly watching the unfolding events.

Are they angry with each other? Or is that Bodhi showing affection for her?

She came to him first too...

She felt that despairing heavy feeling again. Dragging herself out of it, to give a steely look at Kali, she spoke up: "I'm going too, to back up Bodhi."

Charini sensed that, from the sagging expression Ash held, he felt he was losing control of the situation. After all, he was supposed to be a leader for now. There had been no fun days recently, and there seemed to be none ahead.

So much help is required from the adults of the Sangha... I doubt Ash can spare any of them...

Despite the dangers of crossing to the city... there would be three of us... and the destination is Kali's home...

Ash must have been thinking along the same lines. He finally agreed.

After having built herself up, Charini's confidence fast fell away again. *I can't believe what I've just done; I am such a total idiot, as usual... so idiotic. We've just committed ourselves to a journey into ever-increasing danger.*

This strange girl... for Kali she'd be returning to her past life, but... for us... children of a Rural Tribe, out there? Would we be safe with her?

She then thought of the predicament of Bodhi's mum, Dohna, and even Tylanni. She had no real family, but parts of her life were reflected through these people. They gave Charini her identity.

She would find it to be an excursion into a far wider world than she could ever have imagined – lingering remnants in a world that refuses to stop turning.

Part Two

-

Contemporary Family Life

"It wears me out. I want to protect my rules for what a good life was supposed to be, but reality keeps giving me new hurdles and changing its own rules... balancing views I need to hold, of people and situations being either good or bad... it's all so much effort...

Suppose also that, despite most of our good separate intentions, the summation of all our work is an unfortunate result. If we're all striving for competition, especially if our innate needs are already satisfied, then how could the result be anything else?

Has our technology really come so far? Have we really achieved much since our ancestors learnt the land? Sometimes, regardless of how good or how bad my heart feels about it... there are times when tough choices just have to be made..."

1. DESOLATE

Bodhi has previously stepped outside of their home and seen some of this before, but he finds the expanse of this devastation unbelievable. Originally it must have been a massive pine forest. Many trees have been logged, and the rest must have just been in the way. There are no treetops higher than the old logs, and the hillsides of the valleys they cross are bare. The ground too has an odd weight underfoot; a combination of the uppermost soil exposed to the sun, twisted dead material, mushy sawdust and possibly new growth.

Ahead of him he can see Kali leading them. They are following an old path that has weeds growing across it. Using some of the more-often-used tracks might have led to unwanted encounters.

Kali has said it is called a naginata – her long wooden staff that continues into a long blade, which ends in a curve. She has been given back her weapon by the Sangha and Bodhi can currently see it clearly since Kali is using it as a hiking stick. Earlier he noticed that where the blade joined the staff there was thin metal covered in a twisting artistry. According to her, this type of old weapon is from another country, and in peacetime it was used in school sport. City Raiders now use them again for their more dangerous aspects.

Kali wears her old City Raider clothes again. She said that in the Outer Rim, Rural Tribe clothes will make them stand out, but because she is with them, there might be less of a chance of being treated as suckers or faced with aggression.

She does, however, wear a long, hooded, lightweight khaki cloak of a Rural Tribe. The Sangha have given one to each of them to help shelter from the sun, wind and rain whilst walking and sleeping.

Bodhi peeks down at the clothes he wears, as he and the others plod along the path. *The Sangha... everything feels different now... of longing sadness.*

You read a long story or watch a series of videos. You become in love with the characters and story. You have become so involved, they are your friends...

Then it all ends. You miss them. You know that it is final, it isn't real, it won't be continuing.

This is real though...

Bodhi detects Charini falling behind and stops, waiting for her to catch up.

He sees her face. *Maybe she might be... thinking of home too?*

"I'm sure we'll get the illness cure back... with plenty of time to spare," he says, rubbing her arm. Charini flinches and gazes up at Bodhi with such forlorn eyes that he feels the need to reassure her further. "The Sangha will rebuild."

Charini appears to stammer in slight confusion. "But... even then... it won't be the same."

"No... it won't... I guess nothing's permanent..." Bodhi is torn. *I should accept it, I guess... but I don't want to feel this way.* "That goes for the bad times too though."

Charini heaves an enormous sigh and casts her eyes away from Bodhi. He knows her too well and to him she appears to be feeling quite unsure.

He then looks to Kali walking ahead of them. Like Charini, he's also not feeling completely confident; amongst the many unknowns, there is this person leading them, who is basically a stranger.

He senses that Charini has detected his gaze. Checking back with her, he finds she is now also looking to Kali, seemingly fixated in a sullen expression. She calls out to the girl: "Where are we going? Is this really the right way?"

Kali pauses, as if her rhythm has been interrupted, and doesn't bother turning to speak. "I didn't need you two to come along," she delivers in a low voice.

"I only wanted to know..."

Kali spins around. Her expression appears to be extremely flustered. For a moment the girl opens her mouth like she is going to say something, but then stops to collect herself. "We're headed on a longer route around the salt plains to the north of the Outer Rim. It'll avoid us getting too close to the City Centre."

"Oh. Er... what's with the City Centre?" he hears Charini continue.

Kali sighs impatiently. "Even in daylight, it's not a place people go to unless they have no choice. The Centre is the deserted area – it died long ago. Why on earth do you think it's called the Outer Rim?"

Charini falls silent, apparently holding her tongue.

Bodhi's memory perks up. "I seem to remember reading a related poem about seven devils..."

"Yeah, poets can't get enough of the Centre. Some superstition from somewhere."

"I don't know it," says Charini gingerly.

Bodhi expects Kali to explode at hearing another question, but instead she climbs atop one of the logs that encircle them and smirks as she eyes Charini, as if watching prey. She begins to recite the poem and every few syllables she leaps to a new log:

"Seven devils atop tall twin towers
Watch me sin away my fruitful hours
Knowing my folly, they come for me
Enslaving my soul in my melancholy."

Charini puts her hands on her hips and averts her eyes from the display, but Kali continues regardless.

Bodhi admires Kali's leaps. While still holding her staff by its centre, her exacting movements give a clear indication of her training. With each leap the ends of the staff glide through the air in intentional smooth arcs.

A memory suddenly comes to him in a flash – he has seen Kali using her naginata previously, using these skills. *She was trained in these moves with the capacity to kill.*

These thoughts are dispensed quickly though; Kali leaps to her last log and straightens to a stop, like something in the distance has caught her attention.

"What is it?"

"Mmm. Something I thought I'd seen a while ago too."

"Huh?" says Bodhi, and he climbs atop the log to join her. "Where am I looking?"

"That hillside we came down half an hour ago. The same path."

He scans the hillside but finds nothing.

"What is it Bodhes?" Charini asks him worriedly.

He is about to say he sees nothing, when he spots movement. Someone is coming down the opposite hillside at a decent pace. At this distance he can tell nothing about them, except for the hood they are wearing.

"Someone in a black hood with yellow edging... Just someone following the same path?" asks Bodhi.

"I don't think so," says Kali. "I only found this by accident whilst we went cross-country. See? It's not really used."

"Why didn't you say something before?"

"There was nothing to say about it yet," retorts Kali, displaying her annoyance, but without averting her eyes from their quarry. "But they're gaining on us."

Bodhi gazes down at Charini but they just stare at each other. Concerned faces with nothing to say.

Kali continues watching the person in the distance. "Let's get off this path. Now."

~

The cold night had descended hours ago and Bodhi, who is alone, finds it very chilly.

They had waited with baited breath for an hour but nobody had come along the path. Had they evaded the person? It could have been a simple misunderstanding, but dangers were known to roam outside of the city limits. The nature of the hooded person, and what had happened to them, was unknown.

It had become close to dark and Kali had said that if they camped for the night then they'd still reach the Outer Rim later the next day. So they had stayed where they were, hidden between some logs, to safely rest for the night. Bodhi was chosen to be the first to stay up and keep watch, whilst the two girls slept.

Behind him, over where the girls are sleeping, he hears a sigh. As he turns to look, he hears Kali's breathing coming broken and uneven. Seeing the way she is currently twitching as she sleeps suggests to Bodhi that she must be having a bad dream. *Charini had mentioned Kali having nightmares...* Bodhi conjures countless guesses for what she is dreaming about, but soon gives up.

She hasn't gone back over the death of her brother much... From what I know, he was all she had... I wonder what has happened in the past for her to so easily shut herself off...

If I lost Mum...

Bodhi blocks that thought out. *I don't want to see where ideas like that go... Especially with all we've got ahead of us...*

He then recalls his anger at feeling betrayed by Kali, and realises it seems to have subsided. She is potentially a traitor, to either party, but he realises that he now partially ignores it. Regardless of what previously happened or how she felt then, she definitely seems to be helping the Sangha and the other wounded City Raiders now. *Or am I ignoring it because we need her help? Kali's fighting spirit seems innate though... as long as she feels the cause is right...*

Bodhi wants to sneak over to them, to make sure that she and Charini are properly rugged up in their cloaks. He doesn't move an inch though.

He recalls what Kali said earlier, as they gathered weeds to make a bed: *"And don't you try anything creepy whilst us girls are sleeping!"*

Maybe I should find my own spot to sleep... when it comes my turn... so we don't feel too nervous... so that I... don't.

Maybe Kali could do with a longer sleep anyway... He decides to continue his watch for longer than his turn.

Returning to his musing, he then ponders again a strange object he found earlier in the day.

They had come across some rows of laid sandstone bricks that were heavily obscured by weeds. Since the rows intersected to form rectangles, Bodhi assumed this was the crumbling base of what was previously a building.

Likely everything belonging to the place had been salvaged by people over time, but there was something, which Bodhi discovered, that might tell a tale of the wall's history: one very large brick in the corner had a slightly-legible worn inscription. It read: "General Store. This keystone was laid by the Mayor of Mount Torrens, on this day, the 20th of March, 1836." *Very old indeed.*

Kali had told him to hurry up and, as he was about to get moving, Bodhi spotted something sticking out from a mound of dirt near one wall. Digging around it, he finally managed to pull it from its dusty grave.

It was extremely weird, and came in two parts attached together by a curly cable. Bodhi suspected it might have been a phone, since one part had what might be a mouthpiece and an earpiece, and oddly the other larger part had numbers listed around a strange dial. Its scratched cream-coloured plastic didn't seem to be something as old as 250 years ago but it was clearly too large to be like Kali's mobile, and even had another long cable and plug coming out from the larger part.

~

Bodhi hears a disturbance nearby him but it is okay, it is Kali crawling up to him. She has her cloak wrapped tightly around her head and body.

"You didn't wake me."

"It's okay... I felt... I still had the energy."

He doesn't feel the need to say that he has seen nothing so far. In fact, visibility is very low, and all that he has ever been able to make out is the black outline of many twisted logs with the very dark blue hills behind them. With not much moon to light anything, it is the brilliant array of stars that shine bright.

"You want me to hang for a sec, to keep you awake?" asks Bodhi.

In the starlight, he sees a scowl on her face, likely meaning no. Bodhi moves to crawl back to an area near where Charini is sleeping but Kali interrupts him.

"Bodhi, stay up with me for a bit, won't you?" he hears her say in a soothing quiet voice.

He is temporarily surprised and looks toward her. All he can say is "Ah." Bodhi can now only see the silhouette of her covered head against the night sky, but his mind's eye still recalls Kali's soft features and long lashes.

His reaction must have been visible to her though, because she gives a little giggle. "What were you expecting, huh 'Bodhes'?" she teases.

"Humph," Bodhi grunts, not amused. "But if we need to guarantee it..."

"Of course I can stay awake," she says almightily, as Bodhi returns to her.

Instead of sitting up like he's been doing for hours, he lays back to view the stars. She stays seated next to him, the dim moonlight now cast on them both, hugging her knees in the cold and wearing a sly smile.

This darned girl... I like to think I do, but I really don't know what is going on in her head... let alone mine sometimes...

"Kali," he asks. "What was it you were about to tell me... when the City Raiders returned to the Sangha?"

"Nothing." The smile vanishes.

"Really?"

"Yeah. Nothing important," she grumbles.

He gives up on it, although, looking up at her from behind, she has turned her head partially to him and looks to be in thought. He isn't going to push her. Kali walking out on a conversation, as she is known to do, is one thing... but her giving up on finding the cure is something much worse.

"We'll be back in the Outer Rim soon," she says eventually.

"Yeah... are you looking forward to... being home?"

"Not... really," she says in an atonal voice. She seems to keep on musing and isn't scanning the hills anymore.

She has that faraway look about her again... Is she thinking of things past or... Hmm. Her brother?

She doesn't seem afraid... More like a deeper wariness.

I'll ask her another time...

But then Kali continues: "I... don't really think of it as home. Fate seems to keep me on a short leash, like, moving me about really."

"You do... have your own unique strengths though."

Kali hugs her legs tighter, with her chin on her knees. Bodhi can see that her face is now focused above the horizon, so he gazes up at the stars again.

In this deserted region the visible field of stars is huge. The cloudy arm of the Milky Way billows out in a glittering trail across the sky. Bodhi feels small.

"Bodhi, do you feel..." Kali says, "that all of us, we're essentially alone?"

Bodhi thinks to look for the stars that make up the galaxy's clouds, but all he eventually ponders is lonely space dust.

"Bodhi?" whispers Kali. Her face comes into view, as if from a dream. "You're falling asleep; you should go get some rest."

As he hazily crawls back to where Charini is sleeping, Bodhi is impressed to see something he has never seen before – a faint glow of light above the horizon. It must be coming from their destination – the Outer Rim.

~

Drifting out of a heavy slumber, Charini is shocked to find a body looming over her. She is about to give a yelp when the person notices and moves forward suddenly. It is Kali, holding a finger to her lips to be quiet.

"It's your turn to take watch," Kali whispers to Charini's quiet dismay.

Charini groggily rouses herself and blankly follows Kali away from the nook of logs where they have slept. As she looks back to see Bodhi, she realises that him coming in to sleep hadn't disturbed her at all. He looks peaceful, and remembering him showing his care for her earlier in the day makes her heart feel warm.

"I'll hang around for a bit, so you don't fall asleep," says Kali.

"Gee, thanks," says Charini grumpily.

As she follows Kali away from the logs, for some reason she recalls her desperation as she watched Bodhi's admiration for Kali's acrobatics. Charini sighs; she just doesn't have the strength to go over the situation, and running off into the wilderness is a bad idea.

They sit there saying nothing to each other, with their frosty breaths the only sounds to be heard.

They don't have much farther to go on their trek, so Charini's mind is now on the unknowns that are ahead of them. She's seen differing unrelated websites of the city on the Internet, but doesn't know much else. Church groups, products for sale, folk in stylised bars, beauty surgery... What she does know, she feels is simple to comprehend – the City Raiders attacking the Sangha for food. What it means to her is that they are either desperate from being overloaded or have poor land, or are even more horrible... She can't help picturing the place as an overcrowded garbage dump.

Eventually, Kali raises herself to go to bed.

"Kali, when we get to the Outer Rim, where will we be sleeping?"

Kali sighs. "I know of a few people's places."

"Ah, okay. Oh, so not your place?"

"Not if I can help it."

It is quite obvious to Charini that Kali doesn't let people get very close to her. It worries her. *People's lives are at stake here...*

"Kali, please. At least tell me where we're getting the cure from."

Charini can't quite see Kali's face in the darkness, but by the long pause she assumes that Kali isn't happy.

"Fine then, if you really want to know?" Kali says curtly. "I have no idea. The cure existed when I was little, and I have no idea where to find it."

2. URBAN LOOP

"Wow!"

Enormous windmills. Masses of them, like daisies on a bush.

"It so cool!" he hears Charini exclaim. Without taking her eyes off them, she sits down at the crest of the hill with an exhausted exhale.

Bodhi is slightly dumbfounded, and finds it futile to count how many he sees covering the valley and the opposite hillside. "How many... are there?"

"Who knows? At least a few hundred," responds Kali with disinterest.

"Does the Outer Rim... really generate... this much electricity?"

"Of course," Kali says with a grin of superiority, her eyes closed and her arms folded. "There are many people to supply services to, y'see."

Bodhi is taken aback. Not by how many there are, but by the assumption of how much electricity the Outer Rim needs. Especially when he has heard that other power sources are used, such as coal and huge mirror arrays that focus the heat from the sun.

After finding their first building and unsealed road, the trickle of houses steadily increases as they progress. Many buildings are of differing types, but they are often made from red bricks. It is seldom that a house is made entirely from the same colour of red brick – most appear to be made of many tones of red. Some houses also have their own windmills.

The occasional vehicle passes. Most appear to be made from all sorts of mismatched components.

Finally, Kali pulls to a halt and the others do likewise. "Mmm, this should be enough."

"Enough for what?" Bodhi feels they haven't made it very far into civilisation yet – they are seldom meeting a single person on the road.

"The Internet. The Wi-Fi of the Outer Rim Lowlands." Kali flips open her mobile phone and starts plugging away.

Charini's unsure voice pipes up. "What are the... Lowlands?"

Kali's eyes don't leave the screen of her phone. "Unless you're rich enough to live on the Rim, then everyone lives in the lands below."

"Ah. Is there something... in particular... you're looking for?" asks Bodhi.

"Quit bothering me, I'll let you know in a moment."

Charini has already told Bodhi that Kali doesn't know exactly how to find the cure for the illness. In her concern, she was surprised when it didn't shock Bodhi one bit. He has slowly become accustomed to the situations that surround Kali.

It has already been a while, and Kali doesn't look like she will finish any time soon.

"So, found what you're looking for?"

"I said..." Kali growls as she keeps plugging away. "Dammit!"

She slowly withdraws her eyes from her phone, holding its screen against her chest, then looks around at their surroundings. "Let's keep going this way for now."

Bodhi and Charini glance at each other.

~

This is not the place I dreamt of.

The streets are very clean and there are no bins anywhere. By seeing more and more buildings, people's clothes and vehicles, Charini can tell that the Outer Rim recycles as much as possible. Occasionally a wholly manufactured item can be seen, like a car that is brand new, but she assumes that these are likely owned by the wealthier residents.

Charini feels a bit claustrophobic. They are now passing through a market that sells anything she could imagine. Not just completed items, but every spare part a person can dream of. Electronics, mechanical parts, building materials, buttons for clothing. People are using very large wads of old brightly coloured plastic cash in exchange.

Questions are in everything that the Rural Tribe teenagers see.

They exit the markets into a street where the buildings look rock solid, and a few levels high rather than just at ground level. Bodhi starts noticing more people wearing very similar outfits. *How strange.... Can so many people work in the same job? It must be important... especially since they also look very clean... and the clothes must have taken ages to tailor. So many doing the same thing... Grey People, wearing grey jackets and white shirts with trousers or skirts...*

Power lines are strung everywhere in the air between buildings. Bodhi feels that they are in such a mess that he assumes they must have been put there by numerous different groups. *Maybe even individuals themselves?*

So many people, so many houses and streets. *How many stories have travelled these worn roads, this ever-evolving man-made environment?*

This is no medieval society... completely unlike I thought... I had such a poor imagination of the people's intentions. They're using so many ways for life to be kind to the world...

Cars continually pass them on the street, whilst the concrete footpath is full of people.

But it's so overwhelming, especially with those not in a position to make a choice... So many people, so over-engineered...

His thoughts lead him home.

He then pictures what he himself must look like to the people of the Outer Rim. A strange person in an environment of a different style, different motivations.

It must have been similar to how that man felt... A man sitting on his own by a fire, his head covered in black and white cloth. Stared at by others, like Kali and himself.

"Hey Charini?"

"Oh, yes?" He can see that her eyes continue darting about herself too.

"Did you see that old nomad recently? He was alone at the Sangha's campfire one night... before..."

"Nope, sorry."

Bodhi dreams of the man and his family, slowly trekking the desert's sands, with little to hold them down. In the evening, they would be camped near a water hole that had few trees, and tell stories to the children around a campfire.

"What do you think he might have felt?"

"Huh? I didn't see him. I wasn't there, sorry."

"Like... about being in a different place... like ours?"

"I guess," Charini looks to the sky. "He might have found our crops very plentiful compared to what his folks come across."

"Do you think... he was jealous?"

"I... don't think so. Those kinds of people are happy to stick with their own ways, aren't they?"

Bodhi briefly imagines the nomads having fun well into the night, after the children have tired, until the noise of the real city around him suddenly reminds him of where he is.

~

As they continue to venture further into civilisation, the throngs of structures and people steadily increase. Especially the Grey People. That feeling of being enclosed slowly gets worse for Bodhi, and it is becoming harder to stay walking abreast of one another without having to weave around oncoming pedestrians.

"There are a lot of people moving fast the further in we get – is everything okay?" asks Charini.

"This is normal for near sundown. It's Rush Hour," states Kali like they should have known.

"It's... Rush... Hour?"

"Ah, the same happens at sunrise. Each person heads to and from work around the same time, so it creates a bit of congestion really."

"People sure work a lot here," says Charini, twisting past a woman carrying a suitcase. "Back home, we only need to work a few hours each day!" She is almost yelling by the end, as she is starting to fall behind the others.

They keep weaving through the crowd.

"You two are lazy," says Kali eventually.

As it becomes twilight, lamps on tall poles in the street light automatically. Rush Hour almost disappears as most people head indoors before the sun's warmth leaves the air. That is also where they themselves are headed; at this hour Kali has said they might find some information, and a meal, at a place where people meet after work.

"And here we are!" proclaims Kali gleefully as they round a corner.

The street opens out into a large square. Bodhi glimpses a building with a sign that says "Coop's Bar", but he is suddenly pulled back behind the corner by the wrist. Kali is holding onto him, with her other arm barring Charini behind her.

"Wait a second..." she whispers as they hang in the shadows. "I thought it seemed quiet."

As they peek around the corner, Bodhi can see a man has exited Coop's garbed in what appears to Bodhi to be a bullet-proof military vest. He has a large white crucifix crudely painted across the front of it. Atop his head is a triangular black hat, squared off at the top, with a very wide brim.

"He's what everyone in the Rim these days is calling a Raider of the Rapture," Kali says hoarsely into his ear. "They're Christian but not like normal religious folks though – extreme, off-kilter. They're not sanctioned like Raiders either... I don't really understand it, what is actually driving them... They even attack the Outer Rim Lowlands."

"Dangerous huh?"

"I've never seen someone like that in combat, and wouldn't wanna be around when it happens... They lost their way a long time ago, I reckon."

At that distance, Bodhi can't make out much else at all due to the shadows cast by the man's hat, since he now stands under a shimmering street lamp. However, a glowing orange point becomes apparent from what is likely a lit cigarette.

Can he see us? He's facing our direction and not moving. He dares not move; none of them do. The thought of being watched is all in Bodhi's mind, as the man suddenly turns to his right and disappears down a side alleyway.

Bodhi and the others relax, and they aren't the only ones; music starts in Coop's Bar and a din of voices begins to get louder, battling to be heard above the music.

"Great!" says Kali excitedly, launching herself in the direction of Coop's. "Let's go."

After coming through the front door Bodhi finds themselves atop a staircase and are instantly greeted with a view of the floor below. Long polished wooden tables have all kinds of men and women grouped about them – some chatting, some laughing, and a few even occasionally singing or yelling. Some are eating dinner and many are clutching large mugs of drink. Bodhi occasionally detects a number of people glancing at them, but most return to whatever preoccupies them. The flight of stairs leads them down to the stylised grey slate bar that sides the room.

"Kali, some of these people are giving us odd looks," says Charini, looking about herself.

"Two Rural Tribe kids – here – wouldn't you?"

"I don't feel safe here."

"They may have noticed you, but most of their stares seem to be levelled at me." Kali motions them closer. "Some of them have probably already heard about the fiasco at your farm via social media."

"What's social media?"

"It's... ah... I'll explain it another time. Maintaining an online extension of yourself."

"Sounds... painful?" says Charini.

Kali isn't really listening to her though. "Right! Let's get us some malt! You have to have some."

"Sure," says Bodhi, who is more preoccupied with taking in all the goings-on around him.

Charini looks at Bodhi with apprehension. "Ah, I... I'm not sure if we're really supposed to be spending the money the Sangha gave us on this sort of thing."

"We'll be fine. A bit won't hurt."

It doesn't matter how Charini feels, as Kali has already left them for the bar without waiting for a response.

Whilst waiting for her return, Bodhi can't help overhearing the conversations around him. Some are bemoaning a hard week's work; others are assessing their life goals. One young man is talking up an idea with his friends, about a new innovation he has in mind that will lead him to riches. They aren't quite so sure, and neither is Bodhi.

The sound of a blasting TV can still be heard over the din of conversation, which Bodhi's mind only collects in snippets:

"... are suspect of scientific research pointing to impending shortages... Governors have assured us that they are regardless taking strict measures to safeguard the..."

Kali soon returns to them with three mugs. They have droplets of water condensing on their outsides. The base of each mug is quite wide and, as Bodhi accepts his, the weight of it is surprisingly heavy. The fluffy cold yellow liquid doesn't have a completely disagreeable taste though.

~

"Ha, and then Bodhi fell on his butt!" Charini leans back from the table to laugh, and loudly.

Kali falls sideways slightly on her chair and is cackling along with her too.

"You should have seen the look on his face." Then Charini suddenly wheezes: "Ooh! It's just like the face he's got on now!"

Whilst catching her breath, Charini suddenly falls silent.

Bodhi sees Kali look at Charini. It appears that her body has become rigid, and her wide eyes are locked in the direction of the stairs.

A man is coming down the stairs. Bodhi cannot see his face, because it is obscured by a long black hood.

The hood has bright yellow edges.

Without facing the stairs again, Kali rises at a casual pace and takes her heavy empty mug with her. Bodhi watches as she instantly blends into the crowd and slowly makes her way around the edge of it. Looking back to the stairs, the stranger cannot be seen; he must have already reached the crowd.

There is suddenly a piercing screech, which Bodhi instantly recognises to be Kali. It is followed by a loud thud. Bodhi leaps to his feet as everyone in the crowd spins around, some edging towards the walls of the room.

The stranger is lying face-down on the floor. Kali has her full weight atop him, holding one of his arms twisted behind his back. She holds her mug in the air, as if ready to strike him with it at any moment.

"Why have you been following us?" she yells.

The crowd has thus far given no other reaction besides their surprise. In their silence, it seems that everyone is interested in the answer. The room is still but the music remains playing.

"Well?" she yells again.

The stranger finally replies. "Kali? That you?" he says in a hoarse voice.

Kali appears confused and loosens her grip. "Yazuka?" She rips back the hood to reveal an olive-skinned young man with spiky jet-black hair. "What are you doing?"

As she jumps off him and he rises to his feet, the chatter of the crowd erupts again and some turn back to their drinks.

Bodhi realises that the situation has become diffused. Wondering if they'll be in trouble, he looks over at the barman. He looks relaxed and is slowly pulling his hand away from a spear that is mounted on the wall.

Kali drags along Yazuka and pushes him to sit down at their table, facing Bodhi and Charini.

"Geez Kali," Bodhi hears the strange new person say as he rubs his shoulder. He looks to be a similar age to them, or maybe slightly older.

"This is Bodhi, and this is Charini."

"They're dressed like they're in a Rural Tribe."

"You got it."

"Huh. Really." From his disinterest, it strangely doesn't seem to be a problem to Yazuka whatsoever.

"Hi, my name's Yazuka," he says, giving them a large smile. "Some call me Yaz."

The duo nod their heads in a reserved greeting.

"What were you doing following us?" says Kali with a stern glance to the back of his head, before then heading for her own seat.

"Was returning from a job up North. When I got home, felt like a drink at my local bar... and before you sit down... methinks you owe me one Kali."

Kali halts and clenches her fists, but then storms off towards the bar.

Left to fend for themselves as new acquaintances, Charini is the first to find a topic of conversation. "Oh... so... what is your job Yazuka?"

"I'm a Raider, like Kali and Rudra."

Another City Raider... Charini feels uncomfortable again about being from a Rural Tribe, but tries to focus on the fact that the young man doesn't seem any more concerned about them than Kali is about their safety in leaving them alone. *Actually, that doesn't really make me feel better...*

Looking to Bodhi, she sees that his brows are furrowed. His questioning eyes meet hers like he is asking her something, but he seems to have made up his mind when then turning to Yazuka. "Uh... sorry to bear the news... but unfortunately Rudra was killed on his most recent raid."

Yazuka goes wild-eyed. "Woah! Damn it." He stares at a spot he is scratching on the wooden table. "It's a part of the job though," he says, his furrowed eyebrows stretching into strong straight black lines. "Wow, glad y' let me know before asked Kali where he was... she can really get a tad excited sometimes."

"I thought the same... she's been a bit up and down since... I mean, more than normal... sometimes in a rut... but not letting anyone near..."

Yazuka is only half listening though. "Damn this job."

"Oh?" Despite not knowing him, Charini feels for this young man. "You don't want to be doing it?"

Yazuka looks up at her with a weird expression. "Nobody in right minds would actually enjoy dangerously raiding people's homes."

"Oh."

"Not much choice. Not just 'cause the Rim has no choice, but ourselves either. Food is just so expensive here, and... only got my grandpa and kid sister, see."

"So you need this job to support them?" asks Charini.

"That, and... well... got a bit of debt owing to those damn governors of the Rim. I guess it doesn't make me much different from most people here, just don't feel great about it.... it's a bit daft but... wouldn't want my family knowing neither."

"Helping them out is a good thing to do," she says, trying to sound assuring.

"Yeah? I may not be such a hero, governors didn't really leave me with a choice. There's so much I feel could offer the world, if it weren't for them. Already had a lot of the necessary skills, and they need to keep the people fed."

Charini wonders how Yazuka already has the skills and how they left him with no choice, but doesn't want to ask. *I wonder how Kali received her job and training too...*

Despite being a Raider, with stern facial expressions and moody pondering, Yazuka gives off a friendly casual air about him that makes Charini feel at ease. *He seems to have most things under control... unless you throw Kali into the mix, that is.*

"You don't seem to enjoy it here," she says. "All these things like debt and stuff... maybe the people you're fighting, Rural Tribes, may actually be your family's salvation."

"Hah," Yazuka grins at her, suddenly brought out of his malaise. "'Don't really know much 'bout that sort of stuff... just what I need to take care of. The idea of staying safe out there seems a bit rough."

Charini is surprised with herself. She's only just met this person. She hopes that he doesn't think worse of her.

Yazuka continues to smile regardless. "Anyway, on that – what on earth are two Rural Tribe kids doing here in the Rim?"

For Bodhi, this sets his mind on alert.

"Ah..."

He doesn't really want to mention anything about the raid on their Rural Tribe to an unknown City Raider, even if he does know Kali. *I'm not quite sure I wholly comprehend Kali either.*

"A bunch of our families have got some strange illness... and Kali seems to think that there was some cure for it in the Outer Rim when she was little." Bodhi then proceeds to tell Yazuka about what he's witnessed of the illness.

"Huh, y'know what?" says Yazuka, his eyes gazing upwards in thought. "Think I can help y' out."

"What, you can?" jumps in Charini, as Bodhi perks up his ears too.

"Well, kinda, I remember a few things from back then."

"Oh, great!" exclaims Bodhi.

"Was just a kid too, and... from what I remember..."

"Yes?"

"It's not going to be a simple task to get."

"Oh," says Charini, sitting back.

"The cure for it isn't herbs or something – it's a man."

"Eh?" Bodhi furrows his brows. *Unexpected.*

"Well, it's a small bunch of people. The illness was widespread, but some people were immune to it. The cure was always synthesised from their blood."

"Oh. And who?"

"Yeah, good question. It was ages ago and was just a kid."

So now we're on a manhunt then... I'm not sure if this is getting easier or harder... at least we know more, I guess...

"Apologies for gettin' your hopes up a bit mates. Anyway, we've only just met, we're in a pub, an' the conversation has been so serious." He starts looking around. "Where's that troublemaker Kali got to?"

Kali isn't too much longer and returns with some malt for Yazuka. Charini feels that the cheery atmosphere of the surrounds has returned quite quickly. Conversation with someone from outside the Sangha feels like a breath of fresh air, a release, and Charini realises she is enjoying her chat with Yazuka.

"More malt!" exclaims Kali eventually, like she is leading a parade.

"Yes please," cheers on Charini.

"Sure," says Yazuka.

"Well, cough up your money then!" vexes Kali.

Midway through some banter, Charini observes Bodhi stand up, and he excuses himself from the table. Despite Kali still waiting at the bar for more drinks, due to the friendly surrounds she isn't worried at all to be split from Bodhi briefly.

Hey, I'm actually smiling and laughing again… and I didn't realise. She glances at Yazuka, sizing him up. *He's a great guy but… then…*

"Where's Bodhi hey?" asks Kali as she comes back with the next round of malt, her eyes searching the room.

"I think he said he was stepping out for a bit, said the place felt stuffy," replies Yazuka.

The drinks are distributed and the chatter continues. Charini feels that she and Yazuka are getting on well, and they rarely pause in conversation. On the occasions when they do, she notes that Kali isn't saying much, just resting her head on her upturned palm and sipping her malt.

"Arrgh, that idiot," Kali blurts out as she slams down her mug, apparently oblivious to what has been happening around her. She is looking elsewhere, and continues: "What trouble is he getting himself into now?"

Charini doesn't take much notice of the slight interruption, and neither does Yazuka it seems, and they proceed to continue laughing and chatting.

Kali struts to the front door and then, thinking of something, holds her head high. *Stupid girl, Charini can't say or comprehend how obviously infatuated she is with Yazuka.*

~

The valley. The Sangha. The laughing happy faces by the fire.
Mum.
Dohna's caring stern manner. Ash being a larrikin. Anzan's cooking.

The malt hasn't gone down entirely well with Bodhi.

He recalls fond memories of sitting on the desert ridge, overlooking his beautifully growing valley. Green crops all the way to the surrounding hills.

Looking out to the desert though, he can see what might come. The slow death, the encroaching sands. Like a disease, it could slowly eat into the valley. He has mental visions of a sandstorm flying past him on the ridge, blowing hard as it engulfs the Sangha. The burning sand stings his skin, and rips the crops to pieces until only desert is left.

Mum... everyone... the deadly illness...

He shakes his head.

Tending the crops.
Shelling the almonds with Charini, us laughing...
Harvesting the almond orchard... with Kali...
...

Like some coincidence, it is then that Kali whirls out of the front door of Coop's. "What are you doing out here anyway?" she throws at him.

As she steps near him, she quickly quietens as she catches his serious expression.

He realises that before he has always felt confused. Now though, this is one thing he feels very clear about, despite everything.

Bodhi doesn't know what to say but for once doesn't ponder about it either.

He puts his hand on her left elbow to calm her, as he looks into her eyes. *So beautiful, like something I've never beheld before.*

She doesn't look away. She is unmoving.

Bodhi feels he can see deep into her heart. This is a place he wants to be.

Kali then squirms, her head turning to face her shoulder.

"No... I can't," she whimpers. She puts up her other hand and is slowly pushing away his left arm.

"No!" She knocks his other arm away from herself and shakes her head. Twisting away from him, Kali doesn't even look back as she struts for the indoor safety of the bar.

"I... I... I'm sorry!" Bodhi watches her retreat, clutching the pole of a nearby street lamp, his beating heart hurting amidst the background of an adrenaline rush of worry. *Was I wrong? She doesn't like me at all. Was she embarrassed? Will she tell the others?*

For the first time ever, he feels that he has offered the most important thing he ever could... and it has been rejected. Bodhi repeatedly stares at the moon or the pavement, until eventually the increasing cold forces him back inside.

3. SAVING THE PEOPLE

The mood has suddenly changed at Coop's, and so it seems time for everyone to call it a night. Charini asks Bodhi what's wrong but she finds he ignores her, and Kali shuts down completely. In finding they have nowhere to go, Yazuka quickly offers to let them stay the night at his place.

The walk home is just as bad – Charini attempts chitchat with Yazuka, in the surrounds of a stiff presence from two mute companions. She is pretty confident something has happened whilst the two were outside before, and she starts to become just as miffed about not knowing what occurred.

Bodhi stops dragging his feet.

Yazuka has brought them to the twentieth floor of a tall apartment block and has paused before a door. He motions for them to maintain quiet. "My kid sister, Mana, will be asleep now," he whispers.

The door opens onto a room that combines a kitchen and lounge-room in one, with large sliding windows on the far side that make Bodhi confident of how high up they are. The lights of other towering apartment blocks are like an orderly arrangement of stars.

The first thing Bodhi notices is the TV image projected within the largest window pane. The TV window is immensely larger than any TV he's seen before in a Rural Tribe, and he assumes it must be expensive. However, it's not the only light in the room, because the glow of the TV merges with a strange very dim light emanating from the walls themselves.

The only noise in the room is the TV, which now has Bodhi transfixed as they enter. A Grey Man is talking in serious tones: "We asked a local man in the wheat business…" The image then switches view to an elderly man wearing overalls: "I think these scientists are just being sensationalist. Who knows what to believe? Like maybe it's all natural, like when topsoil is lost during flooding?"

"Sorry to keep you up, Grandpa."

Bodhi suddenly notices the shape of a body on one of the couches. It doesn't seem that the girls have noticed him sleeping on the wide couch either.

"I've brought some visitors too," adds Yazuka as he helps the man to sit up. He is a stout round-faced old fellow with a large white beard.

"It's good to meet you Mr…" trails off Charini, unsure.

With a big voice and a great big smile, he seems instantly friendly. "Coombe. But I'm Yazuka's mum's papa, so Grandpa will do just fine."

Yazuka quickly motions for him to speak softly, and Grandpa gives a quiet jovial chuckle.

"You know Kali. These two are Charini and Bodhi."

"It's a pleasure to make your acquaintance. Please be welcome in our home."

"Thank you," the Tribe duo resounds.

"Hi Kali," he says as he sets his pleased eyes on her. "I hope all is well."

The simple wordless grunt she gives, as she walks past him, is followed by a knowing smirk from Grandpa to Yazuka. Bodhi sees that, as the two exchange glances, Yazuka shakes his head to which Grandpa raises a questioning eyebrow.

"Okay, you girls take my room and us guys will sleep out here in the lounge," says Yazuka.

"Give us your room, are you sure?" squeaks Charini.

"Absolutely."

Kali pushes Charini towards the bedroom, which is met with a loud "Hey!" from her. Giving up, Charini whispers loudly, "Goodnight everyone!"

"Goodnight," come the replies.

On hearing that, Bodhi with miffed gusto starts rearranging some of the lounge with Yazuka ready for sleeping. *I hope Kali mentions nothing to Charini about earlier on...*

"I wish I could help you, 'cept for my back."

Bodhi's train of thought breaks. "Ah... by allowing us to stay here, you've already done plenty for us Grandpa."

"Yo Bodhi, thirsty?" interrupts Yazuka as he pushes towards Bodhi a plastic bottle he's obtained from the fridge.

It turns out to be milk. "Uh... you want me to drink from this?"

"Sure, it's fine" says Yazuka as he begins tossing pillows to the floor. "Hey Grandpa? Y' probably already realised these kids are from a Rural Tribe."

Grandpa nods.

Yazuka continues. "Years ago, when was a kid, there was that illness cured by blood – do you remember that?"

"Ah?"

"People who were naturally immune to it already. Apparently the illness has returned to their tribe and was wondering who one of those people was."

Grandpa is briefly silent. Meanwhile, the lounge is slowly being transformed into a bedroom using rugs and pillows.

"You're not going to like it Yazuka," says Grandpa softly.

"Huh?" Both Yazuka and Bodhi stop.

"Of the people I can remember, the only one left is one of the governors. Governor George Mansfield, I think."

~

Bodhi stares at the computer screen. "This is taking forever."

Yazuka had told Bodhi that the upper-classes of the Outer Rim rarely socialise in person. Like many people, they meet via the Internet instead. It is much safer for them that way. Unlike everyone else with smartphones, they are apparently able to afford physical implants to be connected to the Internet. According to Grandpa, ages ago people even sometimes used something called satellites to communicate, which had long since died.

It seems that everyone communicates via the Internet and Wi-Fi... just like Rural Tribes do.

They seem to use a great deal of technology here for everything...

He also remembers what Charini whispered to him this morning about Yazuka's room. *"Yazuka has so much stuff!"*

We're still so different back at the Sangha...

All of a sudden, something that has been bothering Bodhi drifts back from his memory again; he and Kali sitting around the Sangha's campfire when she asked him about the nearby stranger.

The nomad...

What he remembers of the man only gives his busy mind even more food for thought for a while.

Still waiting.

Earlier in the day, Bodhi had asked, "So if we can make an appointment via the governor's website... is there a laptop here we can talk to him with?"

"Computers? He-he-he," chuckled Grandpa. "Did you know that many years ago, despite eating total rubbish, not having them kept people healthy because manual work means more exercise?"

"My only PC with a camera broke and still trying to work out how to buy a new one," Yazuka answered Bodhi.

"Oh... Kali, Yaz, what about one of your smartphones?"

"Maybe not," came from Yazuka as he paced the room. "Neither of us is exactly on best of terms with the governors. Maybe should go to an Internet Café, so you're partly anonymous?"

"Mmmph," came from Kali, who was lying sideways across an armchair and gazing airily elsewhere. It seemed to qualify as an agreement from her.

"Okayee," Bodhi trailed off. "Ah, I can do that... We've got the Internet back at the Sangha, and... I'm familiar with video chats."

"Alright," said Yazuka, who then lowered his voice. "Be wary in working with governors though."

Bodhi had remembered Yazuka's response when Grandpa named Governor Mansfield as a holder of the cure. *"Damn it, in debt again!"*

"Okay, I will."

Bodhi now sits in a nearby Internet Café. To gain an audience with someone important like Governor Mansfield will likely take some time. As a governor of the Outer Rim he is in constant contact with the people he serves, and Bodhi realises he will have to wait in a very long queue for the video chat to begin.

However, Bodhi isn't worried at all. He is content to have escaped Kali for now.

According to Yazuka, unless there was a specific reason otherwise, a governor only meets with one person per video chat. Charini was glad because she was still tired from the trek, and the previous night's malt. Instead she offered to look after Mana whilst Yazuka went to his day job, to give Grandpa a break. Yazuka accepted and said she was very kind in offering, but she said it was the least she could do after their help so far.

Yazuka... He's hardly any older than me... and he seems to run the family...

I feel like a little kid...

In fact... right now... there is a huge amount of responsibility resting on my shoulders...

At last the screen changes to a sign that reads: "You are now proceeding to an audience with an honourable Governor of the Outer Rim Colonies. Please wait..."

Bodhi quickly checks his appearance, and decides to move into a position that means his Rural Tribe clothes aren't entirely visible to the camera.

He then stokes his confidence like the boiler of a steam engine.

This is for Mum...

This is for the Sangha...

A window on the computer's screen suddenly opens, and Bodhi finds himself staring straight into the eyes of Governor George Mansfield. From the debts owed by Yazuka, Bodhi pictured him as a greedy glutton covered in jewels. This man looks healthy, has almost-white hair and wears a very neat suit like the Grey People. His square glasses frame an emotionless round face.

"What might your pleasure be today?"

"Huh? Ah... There's some people in trouble and... you are probably the best to help."

"What is the situation? As a governor I care about the people of the Outer Rim." For Bodhi, the man felt like quite a fast speaker.

"Outer Rim? Actually... it's a bit further North."

"North?"

"Ah... Raiders have been injured while attacking a Rural Tribe and... people have come down with an illness... uh... one that is cured... by your blood."

"My blood?"

"Yes."

"I see..." The man's questioning eyes finally move, looking down to his left, before returning to the inquisition. "This is in a Rural Tribe?"

"Ah... yes."

"I apologise, but I am unable to spare the time."

"Ah! But—"

"There's important work to be done and unfortunately somebody has to take care of it." The man before him seems astute in his conviction of his duty to the people of the city.

"I'm only trying to protect ones I love... we need your help... and you're one of the only ones who can..."

"I hear that often too. Let me tell you this: I am responsible for the people of the Outer Rim, to make sure that the population has the services to ensure the safety and happiness of the people, now and into the future. If I take considerable time away from that to care for someone else then I am not upholding my responsibility. Sometimes we need to make unfortunate choices to ensure the safety of the majority of those that we are responsible for."

As Governor Mansfield speaks, Bodhi listens less and less as his depression sets in. *This is going nowhere... what about my responsibility too?* He has failed, and before the conversation has hardly even started. *Maybe then this won't be fruitless... because there is still a chance... to ask one of those nagging questions...*

"Is that why there are raids on Rural Tribes? Can't people live that way?"

"I did see your clothes..."

Bodhi pushes down the shock and the urge to verify what has exposed him.

"I disagree that stepping back into tribalism is a solution, and not everyone in the population could accept it. I see it as a regression rather than progression."

Bodhi is no longer happy with how the conversation has evolved. It is time to do whatever he feels like. For Bodhi, it comes out really fast. "The tribes of old were fine with their style of living because, as time passes, it becomes the norm for enjoying a good life regardless. Who cares about... what you call benefits... of more advanced technology and more advanced luxuries? What else is it doing for you?"

"Ha ha ha! Okay son. There's no need to be riled. I do not have time for a big discussion either. Let me tell you this: I guess part of what I am saying is that it can be hard to dismantle 'the machine', especially when it is normal life for your community. Stability is key."

"I guess... although every person has a choice for their own lives."

The governor pauses in thought and then smiles. "I guess, but how about this then? What if I agree to do as you ask?"

Bodhi is shocked again. He doesn't want to move or say anything, in case he affects this new outcome. All of his senses are focused on listening to the governor.

"That is what I thought. But, only if you do this one thing first..."

~

When Bodhi returns to Yazuka's apartment, he finds everyone there is waiting to find out what has happened. Kali is still in the armchair, watching the TV with her arms folded, whilst Grandpa is asleep on the nearby couch. Charini is at the kitchen table with Mana, having fun with her as they draw pictures on the TV window by gesturing with their hands in the air.

Yazuka stops pacing the room when Bodhi enters. "So?"

Bodhi considers what they have to do. *First a raid, then sickness, then a cure, finding the man with a cure, and now this... this roundabout chase is becoming annoying...*

Remembering what Governor Mansfield has asked for in exchange for the cure, he recounts it to them. *"I need you to locate the whereabouts of some people that are endangering the lives of us all. So far, the information I have says that they maintain a location somewhere within the City Centre. Let me tell you this: These people... these terrorists... are a danger to us all. They bomb weapons factories, certain financial and marketing companies, shops selling luxury items, and even consumer-driven TV stations. The list goes on: manufacturing, construction and service industries like call centres... If you discover their location and I can verify it – then, and only then, will you have your cure."*

"You're a fool."

Kali is the first to respond, and it isn't a response Bodhi expected.

"What?"

"The City Centre? It's too dangerous," she says as a matter-of-fact.

Yazuka looks resigned to his own thoughts. "Always forced down by idiots with nothing but power," he mutters, shaking his head slowly.

Bodhi is surprised at Kali's unwillingness and responds loudly. "Well, we're still going anyway!"

"I've also heard that those people that the governor calls 'terrorists' are somehow like fighters for the people against tyranny somehow," says Kali, also raising her voice.

"And I heard from him that they even bomb the public... killing themselves in the process... because they think it's a righteous ideal."

"Because an authority tells you what to believe, or to fight, would you Bodhi?"

Bodhi suddenly finds Yazuka stepping in between them. "Kali has a point; this is a governor we're talking about."

Since it isn't Kali talking, Bodhi considers this momentarily. Care needs to be taken to ensure not being lead down a path of wrongdoing. "Maybe we don't make good and bad choices at all... and our situations in life leave less room for free will."

"Whatever," says Kali.

He decides to follow the governor's line. "I don't want to do something wrong, but... sometimes bad things need to happen..." At least one thing he's heard from the governor makes sense to him.

"Bad things for good? How misguided is that?" Kali utters dismissively under her breath, and then: "But you don't get how dangerous it is in there..."

That concerned voice isn't going to deceive me. I'm not falling for one of your games this time... I shouldn't be misplacing my trust again. "No, you're right... But you don't seem to understand that I don't have a choice!" *Does she even consider how I feel about different things counts for anything?*

Kali grimaces. "But it's not —"

I can't believe she's against this now... is she shutting me out too, like she does everyone? "Whatever Kali. No matter how much you fight the outside world, it will still be there y'know... whilst all you actually protect are your troubles within."

Kali slowly stands up, staring eerily at Bodhi. He expects an explosive tirade, and poises himself for the onslaught, but she has already cast her gaze aside, remaining silent. Her expression quickly becomes unsettled and Kali turns tail to the bedroom, slamming the door with an almighty bang.

"Bodhi!" scolds Charini.

"I know!" he yells back at her. In turning to Charini he sees her with her arms around Mana. At some point Mana has started crying and he didn't even notice.

"I know," he says more quietly.

He calls out "I'm sorry Kali," but is too ashamed to pursue her.

"Up until now Bodhi," Charini says with an accusing tone. "Unlike many of us, it's you who has been protecting her."

He strains his ears but hears nothing from the bedroom. Bodhi wishes that Kali could stab him in the chest with her naginata and pull out his stupid heart.

4. STAVING LOSS

Bodhi, Charini and Grandpa are walking up a steep hill on a beautifully sunny day. Grandpa has said that if there is no way of deterring them from heading into the City Centre, the least he thought he could do is to show it to them at a distance. Yazuka is off at one of his daytime jobs and doesn't join them.

Looking uphill they can see the mansions of the Outer Rim governors. Their high walls surround large pockets of land that each have a different peak of the hillside at their centre. Rambling fortress-like buildings are poured over the peaks, with no semblance of continuity in any of them.

Occasionally they stop to catch their breath, especially Grandpa, which is fine as they are able to view back down into the valleys of the Outer Rim.

Charini breathes in a large batch of the hillside air. *It's so good to be out of there for a while.*

She's been living there for only a couple of nights and is starting to become accustomed to it, but memories of the Sangha still shock her with the difference. *I can see why it's so easy to fall into living that way, so normal, but when I look at it again from up here... What a pointless waste...*

However, this walk is good!

Charini assumes Bodhi's mind is on the view of the Rim too, but he looks startled when she speaks. "It's like they cleared the whole area and put a few trees back as an afterthought... busy ants in a big nest!"

Grandpa appears to be woken by that statement too and chuckles. "Heh-heh-heh... settlers choose an area for its fertile land and then, when the village grows into a city, they cover that land in concrete!"

Charini looks quizzically at Grandpa.

"Forgive me lass for my cynical view. It may sound like I'm confused with my choice of home but I'm not."

Bodhi doesn't take as much interest though.

"I've seen it before," is what Kali had said as she whirled out of Yazuka's apartment.

She didn't even look at me as she left... Maybe she just made an excuse... because of yesterday... and the other night...

Grandpa glances in the direction from where the sun can be felt. "Come, let's finish our walk to the top before the day becomes too hot."

"Right!" Charini is grinning, looking to both Grandpa and at him. "And I'll be first!" She shoots off towards the nearby crest of the hill.

Grandpa stands but Bodhi is slow to follow.

"Hah me lad, you needn't always stress about such things. When the time is right, you'll know what to do."

"You mean... about... finding the cure?"

"Ha-ha-ha... No, about your girl trouble," says Grandpa with a glint in his eye.

"I..." stammers Bodhi, but his mind comes up with nothing to say. *How?*

112

"I said don't worry so much about it. Come, we're almost there, and you don't want to come last in the race... behind me, eh? Ha-ha-ha!"

As Bodhi approaches Charini at the top, she doesn't turn at all. Her fixation on the view she can see is eerie. Each step Bodhi takes nearer to the crest increasingly reveals an expanse wider than can be encompassed in a single glance.

The instant comprehension comes to him, he hurts. He feels anguish in his heart and forgets his selfish sorrows. The view is just of a landscape, but it feels to him like it has meaning: a wretched situation. Its pain is so mesmerising that he feels unable to look away. The short uphill jog has left Bodhi breathless and now the number of sights before him leaves him dizzying at their distance and uniqueness.

From the hillside of the Outer Rim he can see the City Centre, like an outside view of a failed experiment. In the hazy distance are ghost-like impossibly tall monoliths of the remains of skyscrapers, buildings only seen by him before in historical accounts on the Internet. Some are crumbling apart, leaving their black steel skeletons pointing to the sky. The base of the hillside nearest to them contains burnt-out old suburban housing, but the houses further away look entirely different; not far to the West of the city, an encroaching sea has reclaimed the land, making the housing sparse to see.

I almost forgot... the sea... I've always wanted to see it...

I've never seen so much water... I know I've seen it in photos, but it's still impressive – going so far that it reaches the horizon.

It is still too far away for Bodhi to discern any waves though. The sea sparkles in the sunshine except for where the tides have formed pathways of junk.

Charini's words come out in pieces as she marvels at the scene. "It's... ah... I shouldn't, but—"

"It's beautiful," Bodhi agrees. "It feels so sad to see such a thing... but... it's amazing."

"What's... why do you think the land behind the city glows a hazy pinky-purple?"

"Heh, pinky-purple. The salt plains... Kali said there were some to the North. Not much will live in salt, except for some bacteria... They give it that colour."

Grandpa hasn't raced up there at all. Bodhi assumes Grandpa is smart enough to play his own game and, soon enough, he does arrive. He comes to rest on an old tree stump whilst they survey the expanse.

"It's something to marvel at, isn't it?"

"Yeah." Bodhi finds them both answering in unison.

"...and dead."

Charini appears to hesitate, like they are about to receive a scolding.

Who wouldn't... for finding such a thing so beautiful.

"It really is dangerous in there, isn't it Grandpa?" asks Bodhi.

"Well, I'm not going to lie to you. Its beauty is a warning signal – to the people of now, the past and the future."

Charini remains silent, but Bodhi jumps in fast with what they both want to know. "You were around when it happened, weren't you?"

"When things slowly change, a person might not notice until it's too late... but if you're old enough to remember what things were like before..." Grandpa states remorsefully, as the duo move to sit on the brown grass nearby him. "Civilisations will always come to an end... everything does..."

Grandpa begins to relate a tale of a quite general nature. It is not a personal story at all, and instead is Grandpa's personal view on the City Centre.

Bodhi questions him repeatedly, but Grandpa avoids any inquisition entirely.

He does eventually tell some of how the City Centre came to be as it is – what led only to a dangerous collapse – but still only with generalisations.

From what he's telling us... this would be something not easily forgotten...

It worries him as to what actually happened to Grandpa, and the old man seems to be reluctant to go any further. With all the situations facing him so far, all this new information is just too much. *I can ponder this crazy story later... when I'm up to it... I don't want that in my thoughts if I'm going to head in there.*

It is definitely enough. With all their efforts expended, they continue to sit upon the grass in a mournful reverie. Nobody looks each other in the eyes for a while. Charini picks at the grass. Bodhi peers at the view, imagining all of the horrible struggles that have brought it to its current state.

"Well, I'm going to head back downhill before I get too tired up here," says Grandpa as he slowly raises himself. Half-heartedly, he says, "My old bones are sure going to feel sore tonight! Ha-ha."

With all the extra information from Grandpa, Charini is now even more confused than she felt earlier. "Grandpa, I still don't get it... with all of these bad things, everything so wrong, why do you stay with it?"

He heaves a great big smile, and Charini feels slightly better. "As I said before, I'm not silly, my dear."

Charini shakes her head in agreement.

"I live where my heart is – Yazuka and my beautiful little granddaughter. I'm old enough to have the strength to be mindful of that."

~

From where she lies, Charini can still see the City Centre from their hill, to her left. Charini has eventually come to lay on her belly in the grass, with Bodhi sitting down beside her, facing it too.

"This must look amazing at sunset, don't you think Charini?"

"Mmm." She agrees, but it nags her. Grandpa's words are still echoing within Charini's mind; the missed opportunities of the people of the City Centre.

...its beauty is a warning signal...

It is beautiful, so now that deceit seems almost cruel... and we're going to walk right in there.

...I live where my heart is...

She peeks at Bodhi from the corner of one eye. He doesn't notice. There is the boy who she's known her whole life. They are friends.

In running out of chances... something may be lost...

It causes her heart to thump.

I can't... I must hold onto this...

She picks more blades of grass and feels their roughness against her fingertips.

"I know it's probably not the right time or manner to say this... except we're about to do something incredibly dangerous."

"To say what?" awakens Bodhi.

We're friends, I can't do this.

"Charini?"

He sounds confused, almost annoyed, so Charini changes her mind and instead listens to her racing heart. She blinks, and for a moment a picture of Kali's face comes to her, followed by images of Kali and Bodhi linked arm-in-arm in front of a yellow-orange sunset. Her racing heart heavies and she clenches the locket at her chest. *I must...*

"Charini?" he says more softly. That's the Bodhi she knew. When she tilts her head in his direction and lifts her eyes, she finds him smiling.

So then it just erupts, as she faces the ground, her words tumbling out fast: "Bodhi, I think I love you."

She doesn't hear anything, and peeks at him again. His gaze is cast aside, his body frozen.

No "I love you too" in return? What have I done to us!?

With tears forming in her eyes, she starts moving to leave but something is slowing her down. *I should get up... C'mon, I should leap to my feet... I don't want to be here to hear the worst...*

She then feels Bodhi's hand on her wrist. "Thank you Charini..." he says. They look into each other's eyes momentarily, but then avoid each other's gaze.

Time seems to stand still for Charini for an age, until finally she hears him continue.

"We've known each other for so long... and with everything going on..."

Bodhi seems to find it harder than usual to collect his thoughts.

"I... need time to be sure of myself... as you're so important to me."

So soon after Kali and all, that is...
I'm such a coward.

~

Neither of them starts packing for any trek into the City Centre. After seeing it, Bodhi and Charini don't even speak about how to find the terrorists for the governor. When also considering Charini's confession, the Yazuka residence is very quiet in the early evening. Yazuka has spoken hardly a word since their return, likely since he sensed something is up, and begins watching the television instead. Bodhi does the same, as does Charini, sitting on the floor with their backs against the couch.

Suddenly Kali bursts in through the front door, carrying no bags, nor any other indication of what she's been up to. Bodhi watches her survey Yazuka and themselves, then the lounge-room's surrounds.

She grimaces. "Really, what is going on here?" Kali folds her arms over, waiting for a response, but with all they've been through the stunned teenagers initially don't know what to say.

Seeing her returned, Bodhi's uptight angst finally melts.

"Kali... I'm sorry."

"Sorry?" She splutters. "Uh, for what?"

"I've been a bit stressed recently... and said dumb things I didn't mean... with these tough tasks endlessly piling up..."

Her eyes have started anxiously looking about the room around them, but then suddenly she faces him. "And you're giving up?"

"What?" he retorts. "No..." He wonders what Kali thinks of him. *All of this responsibility is on my shoulders... and the time to act is now...* "Of course not."

"I said I'd bring back the cure and that's what I'll do..." she states, and her intent observation of him switches to one of defiance towards the ceiling. As her anxiousness stabilises into a haughty cross composure, she turns back to him and shouts. "I won't just leave this by the wayside for you two to mess up and let everyone else perish!"

Bodhi feels a defensive surge within, but still frowns in slight confusion. "Well... then let's do this! By 'everyone else'... you're meaning our families and friends... They are still in trouble!"

She pauses, frowning back at him, and bites her lower lip.

"Bodhi, stand up and face me," is all she finally says in a commanding voice.

Bodhi slowly rises from the carpet, his eyes locked into Kali's contemptuous glare. *She's been formulating some sort of revenge for what I said to her... Well, I'm glad Kali's still going to help us... but I sense I'm in for a hiding...*

"You too Yaz, each of us is gonna give Bodhi some super-fast practice and training."

"Huh. Really," says Yazuka as he raises himself with a grin. "Might suggest we go somewhere other than my lounge-room?"

"Of course we're going to, fool!"

Bodhi feels apprehensive about the difficult training that is about to assault him, putting the City Centre out of his mind entirely, but he tries to calm himself by thinking of families and home. *We're doing this for them, for Mum...*

Kali then turns her fire upon Charini. "You, start packing for the bunch of us!" She is huffing again, like this is all an effort for her.

Charini cowers slightly and nods fast. "Is more training for Bodhi right now really going to be that useful?"

Kali stills, her eyes set thoughtfully low. "I don't know. What I do know though is that an encounter of some kind is highly likely."

~

A family wearing animal skins huddle around a cave fire, as they work with stone tools to pull apart the remains of the day's hunt...

A man herds goats into a muddy pen fenced by found sticks entwined together...

After years of the climate stabilising, a woman wearing strangely woven clothes excitedly displays to an eager community the fruit trees she has learnt to cultivate... Her voice is the same as Charini's, but that feels entirely acceptable to Bodhi.

Hundreds of men work together to build a strange stone bridge between hills, their goal being to transport water past the valley...

Very tall sailing ships arrive at a town's stone port, with the majority of the townsfolk there to cheer for the newcomers...

Steam is pouring out of a cluster of bulky machines, with women tending to them as they spew out fabric...

A flash of light crosses Bodhi's vision and momentarily all he can see are numerous intersecting beams of light. He somehow knows innately that these are electrical pathways covering the Earth, passing information between mankind.

As the light dims, he realises he can now finally see his surroundings. He is no longer the viewer. The wind is howling as it crosses through deep valleys of scrap metal to reach him, between hills of electronics and junk too high to see past.

A girl screams.

Where are they?!

Gazing down at the twisted metal pile before him, Kali and Charini are just visible below, their frightened eyes boring into his.

He feverishly starts pulling out metal bars and reams of cabling, as they silently watch. He keeps ripping junk out, but it seems like the girls are just as trapped as ever.

Their wide eyes are still staring, but not directly at him. As the shadows start moving and the surroundings darken, Bodhi twists to see a startling sight. The tall black skyscrapers of the City Centre are soundlessly crumbling, in slow motion, falling towards them.

Bodhi desperately returns to pulling out more of the rubbish blocking Kali and Charini; circuit boards, plastic bags... He seems to be making no progress, and the girls remain unmoving.

I don't care if it's all falling apart, or how useful this stuff could be! JUST–

Bodhi wakes.

He really didn't think he'd be sleeping much tonight anyway.

5. I'M LOSING YOU

I'm walking down a city street – what used to be a street, in what used to be a city. The road is uneven. It has large cracks in many places and, from within them, the weeds are growing tall.

This is the place we shouldn't have come. We were told it was too dangerous to come, and yet... we have no choice.

Plus it's all... so... quiet...

Charini has not seen any people anywhere. The only noise she hears is a cold wind blowing in from the sea, making the weeds bend and the three of them shiver. The colour of everything painted has faded to grey. Walls are crumbling due to weeds pushing them apart. Streets and buildings that once beheld many stories now have only knowledge of the past.

I'm scared... I never thought about buildings becoming ghosts...

Charini can hear echoes of Kali in the background describing something to them, but she isn't giving Kali her direct attention. It is something to do with one way some people make money living there, by slowly performing salvage operations on the City, selling it as parts to the Outer Rim. The buildings that aren't falling apart are being pulled apart.

At least, that is the least dishonest form of making a living there, for those who have no choice about living elsewhere.

She then realises that Kali is actually talking to her. Charini isn't accustomed to it, as Kali usually only confides in Bodhi, although lately she now seems to avoid him.

I'm so glad that Kali is still with us, we couldn't do this without her.

Something left unsaid was also that they had avoided asking Yazuka for his City Raider expertise; he had Grandpa and Mana to care for. When eventually they had said their goodbyes, Yazuka had been quite angry with himself, but Charini kept reiterating how much his family had already helped them so far.

To search the City, they had decided to systematically cover all areas on its outside first and to slowly work their way inwards once they had completed each circle. By this method they hoped to meet less undesirable people, although it felt slightly fruitless since undesirable people – the terrorists – were exactly who they were searching for.

Charini watches Bodhi as he climbs through a broken brick wall before her. *This place seems so dead, like a ghost, but Bodhi looks so brave. I wish I could be as resolute as he can often be.*

Bodhi isn't feeling brave. In fact, right now he feels he is a coward. His outward appearance is due to his mind being elsewhere.

I should have been more of a man... that night outside the bar.

I couldn't say anything... anything to say I loved her... to help her understand... and now it's a total stuff-up.

If I were Ash talking to Dohna, he wouldn't have felt so... obsessed, no? He would tell her without hesitation, with strength...

He's ten years older than me though... I'm a child... I... can't.

...

But even Charini was able to say so to me...

...

Maybe I can build the strength to do the same now?

Ah, but... yes, so soon after Charini's admission...

122

...

I'm a coward...

I...

...am such a mess.

When did this happen to me? I used to be so in control... keeping my mind in check... as the Sangha taught me to do.

I'm so sorry... Mother.

I need to apologise to the Sangha too.

I've been so caught up in my selfish heart that... I've become totally ignorant to the important tasks at hand.

I WILL be more mindful. This is my responsibility.

~

A car has rusted until it is the colour of dead leaves. Stained in black, it leads Bodhi to believe that it has been set on fire. Like many of the others he has seen in the City Centre, it is mostly a skeletal shell, ransacked for its useful parts.

What interests Bodhi though is that it sits on a large field made from the same man-made rock as a road, sitting perfectly within a faded painted white rectangle. These rectangles are arranged to cover the whole field, and a whole multi-level building has been constructed to house multiples of these fields.

Bodhi assumes a great many vehicles would have been able to park here.

Attached to it is one of the largest and widest buildings that he has seen so far. Atop it are enormous red letters, some missing, that spell out 'Werstfield Sh-pp-ng Plaza'.

What occasionally astounds Bodhi about the City Centre, as they have slowly made their way towards its heart, are his assumptions of how the complexity and size of this society's functions might have been managed. *So much larger than the Outer Rim... how could this have been perpetually possible?*

"Civilisations will always come to an end..." It reminds Bodhi of what Grandpa told them that day, when they first saw the City Centre from the hilltop.

"Well, it didn't all happen overnight – the decline in the biodiversity, the land. That began slowly, but it seems faster all the time."

"But what–" He had been dying to know the details.

"Yes, I was there for the worst part," Grandpa had stated remorsefully, as he and Charini moved to sit on the brown grass nearby him.

Grandpa had first started talking about something different, something to do with people and money. Since the Sangha didn't use it internally, he wasn't quite sure he understood what Grandpa had meant.

I felt he was avoiding it though... I didn't know what he was talking about but it was not what I wanted to know... is what happened here so incredibly painful?

"But..." He had interrupted Grandpa again.

Grandpa grunted and cast his gaze away. He hadn't looked his normal jovial self. "I won't say I wasn't scared – everyone was scared." He had been muttering his words, his eyes set low.

"Ah, it's okay for now Grandpa," Charini soothed. "We don't have to talk about this today." She had then cast a stern glance at Bodhi.

There were noticeable tears in Grandpa's eyes. "We can't forget though. So instead of all the *bad things* I witnessed, I'll just say it this way... With no work available and the value of much becoming worthless, the city inverted... it became the most dangerous place to live... people poured out of it, whilst others tried to hold out. By then we'd also reached an environmental and social tipping point – an increase in requirements and the way of life we depended upon failing. Instead of regathering, society fractured."

Bad things...

"So lots of people escaped to the Outer Rim?" Charini had asked.

"What it became known as. Or further," Grandpa had said, eyeing them both. "For the rich, re-strengthening the idea that everyone had their place seemed natural, where the rich knew what to do and some were destined by birth to follow... not much of a reform considering how society had been anyway. With our huge debts, not many of us could stop being dependent on them..."

Bodhi had really wanted to know the real story from Grandpa, what had happened around him, but at the time it had seemed like the old man didn't want to go any further than his cryptic generalisations.

Now being in the City itself makes Grandpa's stories very vivid, with Bodhi imagining these stories being played out in the scenery surrounding him.

This place is so desolate... What I do know though is that they gave up on this place... for their own safety... to try anew...

Plus... most people still avoid this place... including Kali...

That feeling returns again. The feeling that has been nagging Bodhi for a while now as they traversed the City. The feeling that what this place became, what forced people to flee in fear, has not yet left.

As they pass around the corner of another plaza building, to another field of concrete, Bodhi suddenly realises their carelessness, their dazed ignorance, his fears confirmed. Their appearance surprises a group of three people standing on its far side. Of the three, a young teenage boy with a dirty scruffy appearance, spots them immediately and is already sprinting towards them.

His heart sinks, instantly despondent. Bodhi knows that these are people who pour dread into other's hearts, including Kali's. He knows this because he already knows who they are. Not just by what is painted on the boy's chest, but by the square-topped hat of the man he has encountered before.

These are Raiders of the Rapture. The boy sprinting towards them is brandishing a knife in the air.

"Bodhi!" yells Kali to his attention, as she swings her naginata from her back and holds the staff pointed straight ahead, already standing in a combat stance.

An adrenaline surge has instantly brought Bodhi's heart to a pounding pace. His instincts tell him to pull out Yazuka's hollow metal baseball bat that he has stuck through the top of his backpack, but everything the Sangha has taught him tells him not to do so.

With Kali in such a determined state with such a dangerous weapon, Bodhi begins edging sideways to be a safe distance from her.

The other two men have already started to slowly walk towards them. Seeing Kali pull out her bladed staff, the tallest man quickens his steps after the sprinting boy. He wears a knee-length black coat, and from under it he reveals the leather-bound hilt of some kind of homemade lance. With one swift motion he brandishes its long thin blade and stalks onwards.

Bodhi's eyes are now locked with those of the man in the hat, who is headed directly towards him. He wants to stand sure-footed, but feels any way he holds himself to be wrong. Once again he has the nagging feeling to grab for the baseball bat, but he holds back. Bodhi has seen that the approaching man has something like a crossbow on his own back, but has yet to draw his weapon either.

The meeting of their two groups is imminent, and the elder Rapture Raiders break into a sprint. Bodhi is temporarily transfixed, and he can see the whites of the other man's wild eyes, the crucifix painted in white across a bullet-proof vest, the harsh lines of his stubbly weathered angered face. The spell is broken when the man suddenly erupts in a yell: "Outer Rim bastards!"

The distance between them all closes instantly and the man in the hat throws a right-hook directly towards Bodhi's skull.

Charini watches as Kali holds her naginata by its centre and spins it so that each end of the staff alternately blocks incoming blows from the tall man's lance.

"Rrraah!" Breaking the pattern, after another clang when their weapons meet, Kali suddenly moves to thrust the naginata in a stabbing motion. The tall man deftly avoids it, but the tip of Kali's bladed staff is ever-seeking, searching for an opening in his defences to end the conflict.

The scruffy teenage boy has circled her in an attempt to get near for a fatal blow, and her Rural Tribe cloak billows outwards as she turns and spins her naginata like a helicopter to meet his approach. There will be no opening for a weapon like his in a fight with Kali.

Bodhi feels detached from his body; he moves automatically to block in the way he's been taught; the aching pain of where some of his adversary's blows have connected seems like it has occurred to someone else; the speed of the world is a blur.

The other man stops to encircle Bodhi momentarily. "How dare you enter grounds purged of your crimes!" he growls through his teeth, and launches himself at Bodhi again.

Charini has run back behind the others, feeling safer near the building's corner. She finds watching Kali in a full display of her skills bewildering, and repeated anxious moments of danger leave her heart on a roller-coaster of precipices.

Mysteriously, Kali's attackers suddenly seem to hold back, and seeing Bodhi, Charini screams out Kali's name.

Bodhi is being held in a strangling lock. Standing behind Bodhi, the man has him at his mercy by holding Bodhi's baseball bat across his neck.

Wide-eyed and breathing heavily, Kali slowly brings her naginata to her side, with its blade pointing in the air, indicating her surrender.

The man in the hat releases Bodhi and kicks him to the ground spluttering. Distraught, Charini immediately races from her hiding place to help him back to his feet.

The three of them finally stand with their backs to each other, with their assailants surrounding them from a distance.

"Well done... well done," says the tall man, smiling as he sheaths his lance. "Over a little too early though..." he says with displeasure.

I can't think, I can't think... Bodhi's mind has gone past full alert and he hasn't yet completely recuperated after the ordeal.

"I am Lucius and this," says the tall man, indicating the man in the hat, "is Judias." Lucius doesn't introduce the third person, the dirty teenage boy, who continues to look sullenly away. Judias makes no attempt of a greeting either; he just continues to give them a surly stare.

"We are the willing, who have chosen to sacrifice ourselves for a greater good that people like yourselves would find difficult to comprehend." He is facing the ground as he paces, but suddenly stops to give them a cursory glance.

"Women are unworthy of this task," he announces, but then turns his glare directly onto Bodhi, which makes him feel very uncomfortable. "However you today, boy, have shown us your developing skill."

The pacing continues. Frowning. "It must have been divine will that brought you to us, considering our work..." Lucius halts, frowns deeper, and then nods to himself. "You – will be coming with us."

Hearing his final words, suddenly Kali gives an ear-piercing crying shriek. "Noo!" She has launched herself in the direction of Lucius, the blade of her naginata pointing directly towards his throat. "You can't!!"

Her freaked-out uncontrolled combative distress is so great that she completely fails to notice the actions of Judias to her side. With one deft throw, he pitches Bodhi's baseball bat like a spear. It strikes Kali just below her forehead and, despite the hollow bat having slowed over the long distance, she instantly crumples to the ground.

"Kali!" cry the Tribe teenagers, unable to move in their anguish. All they can do is look on.

Judias spits on the ground and retrieves the baseball bat from near where the inert Kali lies. She appears to be still partially conscious, breathing deep from her exertions, but her eyes remain closed.

Judias lifts the bat high for a downward swing. Charini starts crying.

"Stop!" screams Bodhi. "Leave... her alone... I..." his voice croaks.

Many of his recent fears can be left behind, when not thinking of only himself.

There is... something strong... I can do after all...

"I... will go with you."

The men stop in their tracks, slowly relaxing their posture.

"Bodhi, no!" pleads the shocked Charini.

Bodhi's anxiety begins to decrease as he whispers sorrowfully in her ear. "It's all too dangerous for us three... if I go with them... a trek through the City Centre would be safer."

"You're an idiot! A total idiot!" Charini sobs. "You're not brave – you're crazy! Who the Dharma do you think you are? What about us too?"

"Please... wait for me," whispers Bodhi. He starts walking over to the Raiders of the Rapture, who are now resting their hands on the handles of their weapons.

Bodhi looks over his shoulder at Charini. "Please help Kali... Go back..." he pleads.

As Bodhi reaches them, Lucius indicates in which direction they are to head, and the three Raiders then follow after him.

Charini sinks fast to her knees, completely oblivious to the hurt caused by the broken bitumen, and to the injured teenage girl lying not far from her side.

~

Kali wakes. Instantly a shocking pain shoots through her temples, making it hard for her to focus on what she sees. Grey clouds. She is lying on the hard car-park facing the sky. The icy sea wind is still blowing and she suddenly shivers.

Something is on her forehead. Kali slowly reaches for it but a voice suddenly interrupts her.

"Don't touch that."

Kali rotates her head to her left and finds Charini sitting there. She can see that her dirty cheeks have clean patches on them.

"There was a deep cut where they struck you, but I managed to patch it up."

Kali grunts. "Why'd you bother?" she says curtly.

"I didn't have to bother at all, now did I?" Charini lashes out. "But then, there's the illness cure, and..." Charini's voice starts breaking up. "Things just keep getting worse these days."

I know...

"Bodhi's gone with them," whimpers Charini.

I know...

"I... need your help... I need your help, to get Bodhi back."

Kali rolls her eyes away from Charini and turns over, curling up, hiding from her, clutching her fist to her chest.

"Kali!"

She hears Charini cry out and, along with the loud wail of the wind, she ignores them both.

It hurts. The throbbing hard pain in her head is nothing compared to the hurt within, like something invisible has been cut out of her. It is a part of her and is too hard to let go of, but she doesn't want Charini to see her cry.

It didn't matter what evils she'd done in her life. Bodhi had welcomed her to the Sangha.

He cared for both city and rural folk, and their future together. He'd said he felt it for her too.

He was different... I wanted so much not to fail him...

When she lost her brother, he was there for her.

During their trek to the Rim, listening to Bodhi console Charini left Kali's ears burning.

Under the stars, she had felt she could open up to him, she dearly wanted someone to share things with... then he fell asleep.

But outside the bar... her wanting to be held by him, even... to be kissed... too dangerous!

The people and things we depend upon... give us our weakness...

The statement echoes through her mind.

Why did you make me like that — then leave without me?

The victim can only find solace in allowing her fury to reach a fever point.

My bastard father, losing my brother... HAAAARGH! Why do I allow people so close to me, only to get hurt?!

Fool!

Weak!!

But...

...

I...

I... HATE YOU SO MUCH!

...

What we depend upon...

Part Three

–

Dreams of My Past Renewed

"The lion catching his prey does so without a second thought... I think? He knows nothing of the forces of good and evil.

It worries me, that the two extremes are concepts invented by humans to label others for their ideas... Why is it so easy for me to class someone as a bad person, just because their ideas of what to do are different? Is there such a great fear in me of comprehending and living with the in-between, or with no label at all?

I hope, for my sake, and for everyone's sake, that others are putting in the effort when they view me... especially when my mind is at its worst."

1. VALUED BY THE LOSS

It is something often hard to avoid, when she sleeps.

Kali can see her father, looking at her from a distance. He is just standing there, staring, but with a happy smile on his face. His appearance is just the same as always.

He is the same, but something is different this time, and she knows what it is. No longer is he in the usual city market street setting, but this time it is the desert; one she recognises from being atop the desert ridge of the Sangha.

"Daddy, is everything okay?" It is not her current self that speaks. Kali is now only a viewer. She can see herself as a little girl – her voice sounding so innocent – standing amongst the red-dusted rocky hills.

He gives no response to the girl, only his continual smile.

Dad?

He doesn't hear Kali, and it seems that her younger self doesn't either.

"Daddy?" The little girl sounds worried.

Retaining his smile, Daddy starts to slowly turn and walk off towards the setting sun.

"Daddy!" The girl suddenly becomes desperate. He is starting to disappear into the horizon of the desert sands, almost seeming out of focus with the rising heat.

Kali wrenches her eyes away from Daddy and looks at the little girl with horror. A scream rips out of Kali automatically: *No, don't!*

"Daddy, I need you!" The little girl starts clambering up the hillside to chase him.

No! If you feel that then we'll only be left hurt by that bastard again!

"Daddy, help!"

No!!!

~

Charini looks over at a restlessly sleeping Kali, but does nothing.

Their retreat back to the Outer Rim had been a blur for Charini, a dream of reality passing fast. Kali had been able to walk but occasionally stumbled or wavered, and had refused angrily if Charini offered any help. Whenever that happened, Charini couldn't help but sob. When Kali didn't look angry, she appeared very sad to Charini. Charini wanted her to burst out into tears too, along with her, but she never did.

Once they had reached nearer to the Outer Rim, Kali pulled out her Wi-Fi phone, started a call, and immediately shoved the phone towards Charini. "Yazuka" was the name on the screen, and so she quickly lifted the phone to her ear.

Charini had wanted her voice to sound different, but when she heard his greeting she couldn't help but start crying again.

"Charini? What's happened?" came his fast response.

"I... We..."

"Just stay where you are, and make sure the phone's location estimator is on. I'm coming for you right now."

"Okay..." she had said, turning to Kali, only to find her slumped down to her knees in dizzying fatigue.

It wasn't long before Yazuka had found them. Kali had gotten up and thrown her backpack at him, and he had graciously taken Charini's pack too. As they had walked, Charini explained to him what had happened. She realised later that she hadn't even taken any notice of her still-alien surrounds. Everything passed so quickly, especially when images of predicaments Bodhi might be in kept appearing in her mind and causing her to cry again. These moments were then compounded by thinking of all the problems that were already upon them and the Sangha.

The moment they had made it back to Yazuka's apartment, Kali drew herself across the expensive-looking comfy couch and fell asleep instantly.

This is where they have stayed for the past half an hour. Yazuka has ducked out quickly for some more food and apparently Grandpa is visiting a friend of his with Mana, leaving Charini seated quietly in an armchair near a sleeping Kali.

What can we do?

The mantra is stuck in her mind like a looped audio clip.

What can we do?

Every moment we wait, Bodhes could be in more trouble!

The Sangha will be lost soon too!

Her thoughts are interrupted by larger sighs and quick short breaths coming from Kali. Momentarily Charini worries that Kali is in pain from her injuries, but she reminds herself again of Kali's bad dreams. She leans over and rubs Kali's arm until the girl begins to rouse, though she knows it is more for selfish reasons rather than to calm her.

"What can we do?" Charini speaks aloud in monotone, staring out through the TV window.

"Eh?" says Kali groggily, rolling over.

"We've got to get back there."

"Ehhh?" Kali says, raising her voice.

Charini looks over to find Kali has raised her head and is staring fixedly at her.

"Are you whack? There's no way we can go back in there with just the two of us!" Kali dumps her head back onto the couch cushion.

Charini doesn't perceive any force of attack from Kali's admonition. She feels her own confidence is low again and she doesn't dare rise to any occasion as things stand now. She knows that Kali is right.

"And another thing," Kali says, now facing close to the back of the couch. "I'm definitely not risking my neck for that idiot, who throws himself at the closest danger he can find."

Before Charini can consider Kali's words, there comes the sound of the front door opening. Yazuka steps in carrying bags of food. For a moment Charini sinks back slightly into her melancholy before suddenly realising what is occurring around her.

"Thanks for looking after us Yazuka," says Charini as she goes to help him restock the kitchen.

"You're gonna like this even more," he says.

"What's that?"

"I've gone to meet an acquaintance of mine, says he'll come past in the morning."

"Oh?"

"He's a guy who might know something 'bout Rapture Raiders."

"Ohhh, that's—"

There is a sudden vibration and tuneful noise coming from her pocket. She pulls out Kali's mobile, which has lit up.

"Hey, what're you doing reading my messages? Gimme that!" Kali begins to lift herself from the couch, but is obviously hit by another bout of dizziness and slowly sinks back down. "Humph, whatever."

Charini has already seen the sender's name though, and launches the phone's messaging application with an increasingly wild expectant eagerness.

~

Yazuka is placing a ready-made meal into a microwave when there comes a knock at the door of the apartment.

"I'll get it!" Charini shouts. She is feeling apprehensive, trying to hold back her unhappy thoughts, but is bursting with expectation of what she will see when opening the door.

She does, and there he is.

The tall frame of Ash fills her view and the moment he realises it's her, his trademark grin appears across his face. He is wearing a Rural Tribe cloak, and Charini now realises how much the clothing makes them stand out against the people of the Outer Rim.

"Come in! Come in!" she says, pulling and hugging the arm of the young man at the same time. As she lets go, she feels his arm around her shoulders as they walk together into the living area.

"Ah." Yazuka stops what he is doing and then frowns. "And who is this guy?" he says directly to Charini.

"This is Ash; Ashoka."

"Huh?"

"He's from my Rural Tribe."

"That much I can tell."

She tenses her mouth at Yazuka's lousy reception but she hasn't yet heard a word from Ash. *It's not like jovial Ash to be so quiet...*

She looks into his now-sombre eyes, ignoring Yazuka, who decides to return to staring at the microwave.

"What's news from home... please?"

"Tylanni isn't looking so good."

Charini's heart is in her throat, and she is sure there is plenty more coming.

"Bodhi's mum is worsening... Many are... The City Raiders too... Dohna... too..."

She whimpers, comes to his side, and grabs his arm again, tightly. Charini then notices Kali, who has her face poking over the arm of the couch, eyes wide with one eyebrow raised.

"I'm basically on a task for everyone, to speed up retrieval of the cure ASAP and maybe even some new recruits for the Sangha."

Charini considers the ones she loves; Bodhi's kind mum, the lovely Dohna, mischievous Alexis; there are so many, including even Tylanni. Tylanni, near to death. The name Tylanni for her has always been connected to the word 'bully', but who did what is no longer relevant, completely thrown to the wayside.

"So then we have no choice..." It is Kali's voice that Charini has heard, and she sees the teenage girl confidently rise from the couch without wavering at all. "We have to go back to the City Centre," she says with conviction.

Charini can only nod in thanks.

"I can lend skills this time too," adds Yazuka. His brown eyes are focused directly on her, and his expression is serious.

"Thank you so much Yazuka, thank you for your pledge, but..."

"But?"

"You shouldn't be hasty; you have others to care for too."

"Yeah, but—"

"What would happen to Grandpa and Mana without you? Besides, I've got Ash now too."

"Really—"

"Just remember though," interrupts Kali. "My only objective is to help these people. That was my original pledge, and that is all."

If there is one positive thing that Charini recognises about Kali at least, it is definitely the selfless courage to do whatever it takes for the majority.

"Yes," Charini nods slowly. "There's Bodhi too."

Kali's only response is to cross her arms with an air of indifference.

Ash looks about himself.

"What's all this about the Centre? So where is Bodhi, anyway?"

Preparations are made and they rise early the next morning. Charini is surprised when she enters the lounge room and finds the couch reassembled, and no sleeping Yazuka to wake.

A cursory glance around the room lands her gaze upon a blinking image on the TV window. The image is a box with her name on it which, after selecting it, opens into a message. She finds it to be short:

"Now you have Ash, you are right; you probably don't need my help. Good luck to you with things that are important to you, like Bodhi, Ash and the Rural Tribe."

She is unsure. She feels bad that he might be in an unhappy mood, and about them parting ways like this, but she means what she said.

She doesn't want him to be hurt either.

Enough people have been, concerning us, already.

~

Charini is surrounded by unbelievably tall buildings that extend to touch the sky, like an immediate mountain pinnacle. Cracks appear in their concrete, whilst others are falling apart so much that their metal skeletons alone reach up like spikes. From a distance they appeared to her as dead black monoliths, but up close their repetitive empty rectangular windows seem to spew forth plant life, birds, and the occasional feline on the hunt.

They have made it even further into the City Centre than their last trek, and so far without incident. Leading them alone is the fourth new member to their group, a quiet man named Li. He is tall and very thin, and appears to be in his early thirties. Yazuka knew him through some friends, and now they have placed their whole trust in him because apparently he has knowledge of the Raiders of the Rapture. Trust that Charini isn't keen to stretch too far. Just like Kali, she now feels anyone with connections to the City Centre should be handled with care, and has told Ash so in a whispered conversation.

When they met him for the first time this morning, Li wasn't keen on going through any plans with them, and only said that for now they just need to follow him back into the Centre. Not that they have any choice. Charini has been finding it harder and harder to keep her a focus on all the events at hand, and now there are some things she just doesn't care about any more. Since they lost Bodhi, she's been feeling numb, and has started to just leave any decision-making to the others. An absentee observing the world change around her.

As they walk through totally empty wide streets, not only can she not help but look up, but she also imagines how many people and vehicles might previously have packed this area; cars hardly moving, people filling the insides of the buildings en masse. Now it is just their small group, alone.

Charini is amazed by how much cooperation must have gone into building these skyscrapers, but then she recalls that this isn't how they came about.

It was only days ago, but she still remembers what Grandpa spoke of, during their first encounter with this dead zone:

"The rich probably agreed with everyone else, that too much imaginary money kept being traded and the whole system required the constant making of new money for it to continue working... that so much wealth had become constructed from man-made concepts that had become far removed from the real world, where they actually derived their value and benefit."

All these incredible structures around me... and mostly for personal gain...

Her heart eventually begins to ache for the contrast in environments. Not only with the Outer Rim, but with the Sangha. Seeing such a huge empty environment, her heartache is for what has been. *This place is like the desert we dreamily watch from the ridge... that enormous emptiness... of something now lost...*

Home.

So much time has passed already since we set out for the cure... I hope the Sangha doesn't disappear like this place did—

"Aaargh!"

Charini keels over, her cloud of malaise instantly vanishing. Ash reaches her quickly in one deft move and throws his arms around her shoulders to halt her fall.

She peers down. Carelessly, something has caught her foot mid-step, and parting the weeds she finds that she has tripped on a deep hole built into the side of the street path. For some reason it appears as if it is supposed to be there, and she assumes it is for directing rainwater.

"Ohh," she recollects herself. "Thanks heaps Ash."

"Hahhh, sorry Charini... but you'll probably want to put this somewhere safe too."

He places something small and metal into her hand. It is her precious locket.

"Ohww," Charini bemoans, which brings Kali nearer to peek at what she's holding.

Ash rubs her shoulder. She looks up as he continues on ahead to join Li, but then back to the locket in her cupped hands. The tiny chain that it hangs from has broken.

"A bit too responsible to be much of a jerk anymore, isn't he?" whispers Kali.

"I guess so." Charini smiles meekly since Kali is willing to have a bit of a joke with her, and so she then throws in her best imitation of his trademark guffaw: "Ha!"

She hears Kali snicker, giving Charini the momentary giggles.

Kali is right though... there's been so much responsibility... on us... on Ash... it's been tough—

"So... what's that you've always got about your neck anyway?"

"Oh... er," Charini has lost her train of thought because of the interruption.

They both look up to realise that Ash and Li are getting a bit far ahead, so they begin to follow too.

"It's my keepsake... of my parents. They were killed many years ago, in an attack on the Sangha."

"Ah..."

"It was ages ago though, so who knows if officially sanctioned City Raiders existed back then or if they were some sort of other group. I was so young though, so I... never really knew my parents... I have no memories of my own."

Kali has been listening intently, but breaks her silence with the most polite voice Charini has ever heard her use. "May I... see the little pictures of them?"

"Oh, well you might find this a bit odd, but there aren't any in there."

"Huh? So what on earth is the locket for?"

"It's er... hair. A lock of hair from each of them is within this locket."

"Ahh..."

Their walk becomes silent again. Charini eventually exits her melancholy when she wonders about the City Raider girl too.

"Kali?"

Charini watches her as Kali mulls the passing pavement. "I... know nothing about my mother too," she finally says, in a quiet focused tone. "I only know little things I've heard about from my brother."

"And your dad?"

Kali exhales. "If I ever meet him again," she says, as her eyes narrow. "I'll bloody kick his ass!"

Charini is shocked at what she's hearing. She only ever dreams of a chance to meet her own parents, despite her knowing that it is impossible.

"That man left my brother and I when I was little, to suit his own ends," Kali continues, but her sour expression relaxes as she returns to face Charini. "No matter – he's gone now."

Kali looks about herself.

"My brother and I, we were always trying to save money... we'd always hoped to escape this bloody place one day... and the things it constantly reminds me about."

Charini's heart hurts again. There is the building urge to say something reassuring but she doesn't know how Kali will react. It's great that Kali can open up to her a bit, but she knows telling her that will end in disaster.

It's been a bit long now...

The silence continues to be painful, but at least a sense of comfort with Kali lingers.

2. THEY REPUDIATE

Bodhi sits on the stone floor of a large old grand hall. It is a wide open hall with sunlight pouring through massive holes in the once-slatted wooden roof. Huge dirty white marble columns support the sides of the roof, which reach up past small glassless windows near the ceiling. The hall is full of people too; at least thirty young men, mostly sitting on the stone floor, all in clothing of differing states of disrepair.

Rather than inspecting the young men, Bodhi's attention locks onto the deliberations of seven elder men. Having only recently been brought before them, he is keen to know the outcome of their debate.

Briefly his left leg aches again, reminding him of the trek that brought him here, and ponders the small pieces of information he has learnt of these strange men so far.

They had passed through most of the middle of the City Centre the day before.

Bodhi had constantly marvelled at the height of the skyscrapers, craning his neck to look up towards where their peaks seemed to touch the sky. He had been worried that he would trip whilst still walking but he felt unable to look away from their lofty heights.

"See something you like?" he had then heard Lucius comment, giving Bodhi a start. Lucius and Judias had been walking ahead of him, but Bodhi then found Lucius almost walking alongside him, a questioning stare cast sideways at him.

Bodhi avoided a lie. "Ah... I've never seen something like this before..." His wariness aroused, he then quickly peeked over his shoulder. The scruffy boy was still dawdling along at a good distance behind them.

But Lucius just said nothing and re-joined Judias.

Only minutes later and they had reached the other side of the central area, leaving the extremely tall buildings behind them. They were walking towards a very old bridge, which spanned what must have once been a river, but which was now filled with garbage absolutely covered in dark brown mud.

It stank.

Bodhi felt terrible. He'd never seen an ecosystem sent into such a state before.

The others didn't seem to take any notice, however, and maintained their pace.

Lucius then put up his hand for them to stop and suddenly reeled to face Bodhi.

"Do you really know nothing about this place?"

"Uh?"

"Did you find those sights so admirable?"

Before Bodhi could answer, Lucius had continued.

"The beginning of this century was the good days, when Christian might had God on our side. But we fell into apathy... life continually becoming worse, and thinking again that money would save us... Hence... God caused this." Lucius had exhibited the tall buildings of the City Centre by slowly casting his hand sideways in a grandiose manner. "Humanity continually sinned by worshipping economic growth instead. How far did we think we could get on our own?"

Bodhi felt that he was far out of his social circle of understanding. He didn't know what kind of answer was expected of him. Instead he thought that maybe just using what he knew as truth might ring a chord.

"Well... I agree... that... growth forever on a finite planet... it's just not..."

"Hmmm?" Lucius came closer and really did look like he was seeking a specific answer.

Bodhi sneaked a glimpse at Judias, but the man was gazing off into the distance like he wasn't interested. "Uh..."

"Yes?"

"But why don't you... think it's due to... growing populations?" Bodhi spied Judias' shoulders appearing to sag as he spoke, and he saw the man turn to face another pointless direction. "Um... er... like... populations... degrading sources of water and overworking soil?"

"That–" Lucius had stolen himself away, concealing what was already a stern expression. He then appeared to relax slightly. "Pah. That is exactly what those deniers say."

Deniers?

"It being brought on by climate change, soil degradation, and the like, it's all just governor propaganda. Exactly the junk they've been putting out as an excuse, an ex-cuse," he asserted loudly. "An excuse to continue their money-grabbing sins, to maintain the status quo."

"I, uh..."

"Let me tell you a story. When I was a young man, I was training to be a pastor for the Church of the Salvation. As I grew, my turn for taking over the congregation drew nearer with each day, but as that time passed the group slowly became... smaller."

It looked like Lucius had become saddened and, not wanting to interrupt, Bodhi had waited to see if the man might continue.

"We slowly ran out of money and eventually had to sell the church. Know what they did to it?"

Bodhi shook his head hurriedly.

"Poker machines, they filled the place with poker machines! I could not believe it!"

"Uh... What are... poker... machines?"

The man still hadn't turned to face him. "Gambling, they're machines for gambling," he said quietly.

Not often around money, Bodhi still felt he didn't quite understand what the downtrodden man was talking about. "Oh..."

Lucius threw up his hands and exhaled dismissively. "We keep going."

The others followed after him immediately, continuing over the stinking bridge, so Bodhi did the same.

He was trying to avoid glimpsing the horrible river by staring at the pavement instead, but something large up ahead caught his attention.

An old church. He not only recognised what it was from pictures on the Internet, but from others he'd spotted in the Outer Rim. At each corner of its front face were two square tall towers built from yellow-brown sandstone, capped with skeletal remains of wooden spires. At the base of each tower was a thick wooden door, with one larger double-door filling the space between them. As they neared it Bodhi was also able to make out ornate carvings adorning the space below the door archways.

"We here are the chosen, who continue God's great work," a pleased Lucius had announced as he mounted the front steps, and then proceeded to push the main double doors open wide.

The dim light had exposed the wide open hall, the one in which Bodhi now sits. Some of the people had stood as they had entered but, in particular, five very old men had come forward from the group of young men. They looked pale, frail and thin compared to Lucius and Judias but, in much the same fashion, they all wore similar items to them; long grey coats, wide-brimmed hats and worn leather boots. The most common factor was very clear and sent a chill down Bodhi's spine – the white crucifix each had crudely painted upon some part of their clothing.

"Along with us, *these* are your new masters," had been Lucius' only introduction.

It has now been some time since the men began their private debate.

Bodhi inspects the forlorn and, more apparently, slightly freaked-out young men about him. None of them seem to be in a hurry to leave.

Are these... the... terrorists? I don't quite know what is really supposed to identify them...

Governor Mansfield... he didn't really want us to get anywhere... did he?

I guess... Kali would have said something if this was them... having known about Rapture Raiders already... How much did she really know though?

"...they're not like most Christian folks though, or Raiders..."

Bodhi keenly remembers Kali's wariness of these men, when they first encountered Judias. *Why then do they also have the term 'Raiders' in their name?*

The randomness of what might happen next scares him.

Looking back to the deliberating elders, he starts to note something odd he must have missed earlier. The old men. They look tired and are not necessarily taking an active part and, to Bodhi, it seems more like Lucius is doing most of the talking. Judias is standing nearby Lucius too, but he appears to be extremely bored.

Suddenly silence falls and, eerily, every single member of the meeting turns to face his direction, like they sensed his gaze. Lucius stands up and walks toward him.

"We will put you to work, but first... this instance has a necessary step. Follow me." Lucius beckons Bodhi towards the end of the church.

The uneasiness surrounding him ensures Bodhi obediently follows. *There must be some way out of this... This seems to be turning out to be messier than I expected...*

"Our role, here in this new holy land, is an important one," remarks Lucius as they walk. Bodhi is slightly unnerved by the fact that the other elders are following closely behind. "The Armageddon that destroyed the City Centre was the first wave of cleansing, and it is our duty to continue it."

As they approach the end of the church they come upon a stage of sorts, but the walls are very bare. Bodhi assumes that the church must have been ransacked long ago. Something very large though is on the stage, obscured by a large green tarpaulin.

"In building towards a new Eden," says Lucius as he stops and turns in front of the large object. "It necessitates... certain guarantees."

Lucius pulls the tarpaulin with one quick yank, to reveal a strange machine. The dark grey and black hulk is nothing like Bodhi has ever seen before. There seems to be a gaping hole in the hulk from where an adjustable chair protrudes by the head end, and one side has a control panel of numerous dials.

Bodhi's instincts say to be scared, and he is. "Wha–?"

Before he can continue, some of the elderly men grasp him from behind. For men that looked so weak to Bodhi before, the tight pain strung across his tendons surprises him, as his arms are forcibly held behind his back.

"You are to be indoctrinated in the pure ways of our Lord – only then can you join the Army of God. Until your learning is complete, if you try to escape..."

Bodhi returns to his senses and, knowing his situation is becoming dire, his focus locks on to Lucius.

"... we will not hesitate to kill you."

A fast sinking feeling comes to Bodhi. *There must be a way out of this!*

"Your current mindset has been concerning me... One that is often found in the City. Don't worry, we do have this fast route to make it easier for you."

Bodhi is only partly sure of what he's referring to but assumes that he probably wouldn't agree.

"This," the man says as he slaps the machine, "is something we've kept from the good old military days. It's a memory repressor."

"Huh?" His mind snaps and Bodhi instinctively struggles to be let go, he must get out of here, but numerous strong hands eventually calm his resistance.

"Your memory needs to be erased."

What?!

"I'm sorry, but we all pay a price for a piece of the divine."

This whole time he has been unable to conceive of any way out. As they lock him into the machine, limbs under latches and his head deep within the dark metal hole of the apparatus, he attempts no further struggle.

This is because Bodhi realises his gamble has been a failure.

I'm sorry... Mum...

I've... failed... everyone...

His thoughts can only turn to dear memories of the Sangha.

His mum jogging past the potato fields.

Charini lazing under a tree and reading.

Dohna telling off Ash for too much cider the night before.

Sitting on the desert ridge with just Kali, alone... as the morning sun rises, and her quietly searching out the depths of his eyes...

He gazes back, wondering a world of questions and conjuring hope; the disarray of the attacked Sangha leaving his mind completely...

But she breaks away – and her fleetingly anxious brows are then arrested into blankness as she becomes focused on the distant desert sands.

He dearly hopes these memories won't be lost in their entirety.

It aches. *My love for Kali.... Please, please don't let me lose that too!*

A silent tear rolls down one of his cheeks.

~

They are resting and finishing their rationed lunch in what must have been a place for eating, since it is full of numerous round tables and chairs. Charini also remembers having seen a sign when they entered saying 'Starbarks', but it doesn't seem to mean anything to her. The place is at the base of one of the higher skyscrapers and the glassless window-front gives them a full view of the empty street.

"I'm going to try and get myself to a higher floor, to survey for any signs of people about," says Li, and she sees him push some crumbed wrappings away from himself.

Charini raises an eyebrow at Ash.

"I reckon I might join you," he says hurriedly as he lifts himself from the table.

"Be safe climbing up there, won't you?" Charini asks worriedly.

"Ha! These old business buildings look really strong. Don't worry Chaz, we'll be careful."

She isn't quite sure and watches him as he exits through a side door, leaving his backpack with them near the table. Her concern is not limited to just the old building or the City Centre.

Everything becomes quiet fast. She realises that this is the first time that she and a recuperated Kali have been left alone together since their unhappy return to the Outer Rim.

Since... we lost Bodhi.

She doesn't know what to say and, since she knows Kali isn't often a conversationalist, doesn't worry about it as much as she might have with someone else.

Why is she here anyway?

Looking for something to do?
A home?
She knows she is delaying the inevitable.

Events past come to her, visions of moments she has witnessed; Kali hanging around Bodhi with not much to do; something important happens and Kali telling him first. It isn't hard to assume that she cares for him, or is at least interested by him.

Then there's Bodhi. Charini knows him well, and has done for the life they've shared together. She can tell how he looks at Kali when they are together.

He cares for her dearly.
This thought, actually, doesn't startle her.
I care for him too.

Charini starts to consider that these musings don't seem to shock her at all. *In fact, somehow my pangs of potentially losing him to her stopped when he left. Or maybe before. We've all been through so much, I feel much stronger for it, but why have I...*

She peeks at Kali, who is slowly picking at the fallen remains of what has previously been a rice-paper roll.

I had already lost to her, hadn't I? I just didn't want to admit it... and yet, I don't feel so bad about it now...

Maybe... it's because...

She knows, because she feels so absolute about it in her heart.

It's because I know dear Bodhes, and what we have will never be lost. We are lifelong friends. I feel strong in that, for sure.

Maybe it all came on when Kali arrived?

Whatever... it's okay.

I like them both.

Charini wonders how Kali is coping with losing him, not even considering everything else she's lost. She knows that Kali's mind and hers likely operate entirely differently, but she likes the idea of empathising with Kali losing the love of her life.

...and my lifelong friend...

She understands that she's done this to herself, but her heart yearns again for a resolution to the missing Bodhi. *I hope Kali's okay too...*

After avoiding her so far, she finally shoots a glance in Kali's direction. "Hey, Kali, you're feeling okay, aren't you?"

"Errh?" Kali's unsteady voice obviously isn't ready for an inquisition.

"You've been so amazing lately, accomplishing so much."

"Huh?"

"Most of what has been achieved has been due mainly to you alone."

"Yerp, that's my lot in life," Kali says dismissively, her sideways glance cautious of what's coming.

"I mean, you lost your family—"

"Huh?" Kali's eyes widen.

Charini hurries to cover her blunder. "But you manage well—"

"Do I have a choice?!"

"I... ah... you've done so well."

"Look, just leave it alone, alright?" Kali screeches.

"But—"

"I said—!"

Kali casts her eyes away to the side. Without looking, she starts to say something back to Charini again but then interrupts herself.

Charini feels bad for her clumsiness and doesn't want to look Kali in the eye either.

The scraping of chair feet interrupts her thoughts though, because Kali has suddenly vaulted herself up from the table and stormed out the front door.

Stupid girl...

Her exit has followed no plan whatsoever. She halts her steps, and instead slams her back and ends up leaning against the concrete wall of the abandoned street shop next door.

Doesn't she—

Hey, why does everyone think that I'm the one who needs help? I'M not the one we lost now, am I, huh?

The breeze that is forced between the passages of the CBD picks up a little, and an empty can of cola rattling loudly along the curb distracts her from her anger.

Bodhi didn't really have confidence in me either. Same as all the others...

She remembers when she thought nothing of him too, but then later her sparring lesson with him caught her completely off guard.

That determination could be funny, like camping in the wilderness... teasing him... him maybe looking too keen... She smiles to herself, but weakly, then miserably.

Then there were those distant faces he has, when he is lost to thinking too hard... When they had rested with hunger after a long day's work, he hadn't known at all how she'd studied his face, wondering what he felt whilst he pondered over that nomad. *Those continually surprising ideas he seemed to have... and he truly had wanted everyone to be safe.*

The memory of the City Raiders returning to the Rural Tribe comes to her momentarily, but she shuts it out of her mind again.

Outside Coop's.

Him holding me, the electricity I felt when he touched my arm... I could see to the depths of him through those eyes...

...

I pushed you away... and now you're gone...

Also because of me too...

She has no idea what predicament Bodhi might be in now, so all she pictures are montages of him being inflicted with pain.

That often-felt feverish pang begins in her heart again, which cries out for a remedy.

I don't need you! I'll be perfectly fine without you. In fact...

I HAVE been surviving without my brother, just like that stupid girl says...

...

Yet... You gave me something I never had in my brother...

...

She realises that she is rubbing an edge of her woven khaki skirt between her thumb and forefinger. *The others too... These two from the Rural Tribe are not just here for the Sangha, but for you too... They love and help each other...*

It then dawns on Kali that, unlike her father and brother...

Bodhi is not yet gone.

The resolve that she thought she'd lost begins to boil desperately within.

We're wasting time...

~

Why would these people do... such... cruel things? If it's true what Alexis said... that all want love... and avoid suffering...

The Raiders of the Rapture must be suffering very greatly...

"The Lord will thank you for your noble offer to aid in His plan."

Bodhi hears what must be Lucius step nearer the machine, after the others have all finished their tasks. He can hear him tinkering with unknown parts, as all he can see through the cracks of metal is a control panel and Lucius' waistline.

"I'm always impressed with how this works," he hears the man say aloud amongst sounds of pressed plastic buttons.

Not that Bodhi is impressed, in the least. His mind darts furiously to too many unhinged conclusions – he feels worse than what he suspects it must feel like to be close to death.

"There is, however, another very convenient side effect it has..."

Lucius' new information on the outcome is too much to bear. Hearing the man's last words, Bodhi feels no longer in control of his body, he is just a spectator. His mouth feels so dry, too dry.

Nooo! I... can't...

He wants to throw up. His chest attempts to lurch forwards despite his incarceration.

No... that can't be possible... !

He has no chance to be physically ill however – one of his eyes locks onto an image of a hand that belongs to Lucius already heading towards a large red-lit button.

3. LIBERTYCHNOLOGY

"Just hang here a moment mates," says Li, raising his right hand.

Up until now, Charini has stayed in her dreamy malaise, watching the world pass by and dragging her feet.

He approaches a tall octagonal skyscraper that is held up by concrete cylindrical columns, leaving them to wait on the footpath across the empty street.

To Charini's amazement, as Li reaches one of the columns, another man casually steps out from behind and greets Li. He has a large belly, wears a fishing vest and carries a sports bag slung over one shoulder. What worries Charini the most is what looks to be a gun hanging over the same shoulder by a black strap.

"I don't like the look of this," says Kali sternly.

The two men seem to chat briefly, they seem friendly, with Li indicating to them occasionally. Once their conversation ends, Li jogs back over to them.

"What this? What's going on?" asks Ash.

"It's okay, okay. I know this guy. We're going to head into this building now. It's going to be in all our best interests for sure."

"Hahh," sighs Ash.

"C'mon mates, trust me."

"Hahmm, okay..."

They start walking towards the larger man, when Li chimes in again: "Oh, I almost forgot. Your weapons... You're going to need to hand them over to me for a while for safekeeping."

Kali issues only one quick low-pitched short syllable: "What?"

"Trust me mates. It's for everyone's safety here."

There isn't much point in arguing, when one person is carrying a gun.

Not long later and Charini, Kali and Ash are being ushered down a dark concrete hallway by the two men. The large man is leading them and Li is following up the rear.

Charini is glad that Ash is behind her and Kali is taking the front. Warning bells are sounding in her mind. *There are too many unknowns here; we're out of our depth...*

They arrive at a set of double-doors with small windows set in them. The larger man peeks through the windows as he knocks, and a muffled "Enter" comes in response.

What greets Charini is a room of around twenty people lounging about on the ground or standing. Men, women, dressed in all kinds of durable outfits, who all rise as they enter. The room seems to be barren of furniture, but the concrete floor is noticeably strewn with dangerous weapons of differing kinds.

Uh oh...

"Cheers Dr Z," Charini hears from an unseen person within the crowd, and the larger man nods.

She is suddenly shocked to feel someone shove her from behind, and the group parts to reveal two people.

One is a man in a black tank-top and pinstriped trousers, who is seated in a cushioned green velvet armchair. He has grey-white hair and black stubble, with black rectangular glasses that frame a square face.

Leaning with her weight upon one elbow, resting atop the chair, is a tall woman, maybe in her late thirties, whom Charini instantly perceives as very beautiful. She has startlingly red hair and what appear to be hazel eyes. Almost everything she wears is black – turtleneck skivvy, leggings – apart from her denim skirt.

"Huh, so this is what security outside mentioned? It's just some young guy an' a coupla kids," laughs the man. Charini finds his almost-nasal fast-talking voice to be harsh, his letter 'a' sounding to her as if it has been cawed by a crow. "An' a girl dressed up like she thinks she's a government City Raider."

Some of the adults in the room chortle, and Charini hears Kali grunt.

"Ah, she does have this though," pipes up Li as he taps the base of Kali's naginata on the concrete floor, him knowing full well her profession. He lays it on the ground for all to see.

The man in the armchair continues to speak fast, now sounding excited. "Really... So what on earth do you kids think you're playin' at, hmmmm?" His grin has gone and he leans forwards in his chair.

It appears that Li is about to explain, but the man waves him away. His gaze is locked onto the remaining three of them.

Ash responds coyly. "Our friend... he was kidnapped by Raiders of the Rapture."

The two facing them say nothing, poker-faced, apparently considering his words. "How did this happen?" asks the man, leaning forwards. "Can you remember what they look like?"

"Oh, we ah..." begins Charini. "We were ambushed on the outskirts of the City Centre. One guy was carrying a long thin sword-looking–"

"Hmm, sounds like Lucius, that poor deluded man," interrupts the woman, who then re-adjusts her footing. "Look, we are people who are in a position which *might* aid you to get your friend back but... to be honest... it's complicated."

Charini's hopes rise cautiously, awaiting the devil in the detail.

"They're commonly holed up in a place not far from here."

"Wait a moment," brightens up the man in the chair, then scrutinising the three of them again with a frown. "There's somethin'... What were Rural Tribes kids doing all the way out here to get in trouble anyhow?"

He brings his frowning face closer to Charini's, his stern demeanour making her want to shudder and hide.

Ash steps forward slightly.

"And with a governor-sanctioned City Raider no less..."

"Er..." Until meeting these people she has been thinking that the Rapture Raiders were always who they were looking for, but now Charini's renewed suspicions are a cause for her concern... *but they just offered to help us find Bodhi...*

The silence from the trio must have appeared damning.

"What're ya thinking of doing, eh, are you whack?" yells the man as the room then erupts into a loud discourse. "These are all good people here," he says, casting an upturned hand around. "We used to be teachers, bankers, homemakers. We're doin' something for the common good and you wanna go against that?"

"Whatever," Kali bursts out defiantly. "So what's the big secret with you kids playing around out here anyway?"

"Hey, we're asking the questions here!" barks the woman.

"Us? What are we up to?" the man interrupts with a grin. "What are we up to?? *We* are the Neo Liberation Army," he says proudly. "I am Zhu, and this is my wife, Cassandra. And you... are... very... suspicious..."

Charini feels like she is on thin ice, thinking that even the slightest perspiration of worry from her might cause a cataclysm.

"To be more specific," smiles Cassandra, strangely calm again, "all of us here aim to liberate everyone from total enslavement by oppressive or opulent technology," she surmises.

"Yeah, so we can focus on ways to truly improve the lives of everybody," cuts in Zhu. "A Palaeolithic child brought up in today's environment ain't no dumber than us – we haven't come so far. Know what one of them is?"

"What are you–?" Ash begins.

"Didn't think you would. That time was back ages ago humans were doin' work with stone tools, well, it was a really long time ago. Anyway, here and now, part of our efforts is to sabotage companies that automate jobs previously done by workers. You know... manufacturing, construction, service industries like call centres, eeeet cetera."

"Although I used to hate working in a call centre as a teenager, so either way," adds a smiling Cassandra out loud.

Kali casts an idiotic expression at Charini, and feels quite confident she can guess the type of sarcastic comment Kali is telling her. *Gee, could these be the people we're looking for?*

Sabotage. Bombings. These are not methods Charini would hope lead to a better world. It nags her, and the urge to ask "Why?" is strong, but not as strong as a wariness of potential danger.

Zhu is still rambling fast though. "I mean, this is a contributing catalyst for the breakup of society aaaaand the death of the City Centre."

Charini realises she is already far behind in comprehension. "Huh? What is?"

"Requirin' paid labour an' so people can pay for consumption, of course! There are only so many hits an economy can take at the same time."

"I don't..." Charini then temporarily collects her head within the whirlwind. "Isn't it a problem that... people can be paid to over-consume in the first place? Automation can be useful in my Tribe."

"Not if it's nicking your jobs, it ain't."

"Jobs? But..." *Advanced automation technology was the past, right? It ruins people's exercise; people can live perfectly fine without it...*

In the background Charini can still hear Zhu rambling on excitedly regardless. "Isn't it odd that employees are usually told to all work together for the benefit of a company? Step outside the office door though..."

Charini has tuned out. Her cloud of malaise has been nagging at her again to just exit this situation and return to being an observing third party. From the recent days' events, to the situation they are in now, it has all been too much too fast. She's been feeling a disconnect from it all; all that's really important to her is the Sangha and Bodhi. Should she be afraid of these people? Could they be supportive? Despite any of their good intentions, she's not sure where they see eye-to-eye. She understands their gripes, but is the way they do things really aiding the future?

Ash suddenly speaks out in a voice that Charini recognises as him being cocky. "Ha. If living here seems such a problem, then why don't people join us in Rural Tribes?"

Zhu and Cassandra chuckle together, and everyone there subsequently joins them in raucous laughter. Ash looks about himself with a subdued expression.

"You think we're a failed attempt at being like you?" sneers Zhu. "Let me tell you brother, there are many reasons why people can find it hard to change."

Cassandra nods with her arms folded and eyes half closed, like a teacher assessing her students.

Zhu continues. "But, y'see, being in transition is problematic. I reckon currently movin' to a Rural Tribe is a Catch-22... not that you know what I mean by that. It's a good example though... Anyway, well, besides City Raiders, you also have to deal with other groups attempting to move to the same land."

"The Outer Rim governors likely don't bother taking the land for the same reasons, and the Rural Tribes are like free workers for them," adds Cassandra.

"Rural Tribes? Pah. You're only gettin' me started. Instead of trying to be a force to save humanity, you're just abandoning it to save yourselves... Don't you see? Just with hope and doin' the right thing isn't good enough! The sum of us all still leaves everything collapsing!"

"Ahh, yep," agrees Cassandra, facing away like she's heard this often. "Only the will to act can bring us forward."

To Charini's surprise, she then detects Kali huffing. "I've met your type before," the teenager wheezes through her teeth with malice.

Charini hasn't been paying much attention to her until now, and it appears that Kali is far more worked up than she has ever seen before, but she can't entirely fathom what in particular has offended her, Kali being a City Raider and not of a Rural Tribe.

"So much bravado, fighting for freedom..."

Charini touches her arm but Kali seems to disregard her.

"Running off instead of caring for your own children!"

The place goes quiet as the people appear to be attempting to absorb the sentence.

"Er... Do you really think some of us were left with a choice?" retorts Zhu.

"And do you think they are thanking you for leaving them? Huh?!"

Everyone continues to be left in an awkward silence, except for the sound of Kali breathing heavily.

Eventually Dr Z steps in with a soothing voice. "Some of us, young miss, when pursued by the governors, had no choice but to leave our families to protect them."

Kali's mouth gapes and her eyes momentarily widen, before her stunned expression eventually comes to rest in a frown.

"Yah, fa' example, nobody here even knows what Dr Z's last name is, at all," throws in Zhu lackadaisically, waving a hand about in the air.

"It's true," the squat man says, nodding to Kali.

Kali still hasn't moved, and Charini becomes worried. She touches her elbow, which jolts Kali back into the present with a furtive glance to her side.

Kali's actions are making Charini feel quite anxious. She hopes Kali will back down a bit, considering their current predicament; a hope for Kali that doesn't calm her anxiety one bit, especially when she sees the girl mentally reawaken to face the two Neos again.

"You lot bombing, especially via suicide bombers, isn't really helping your cause y'know, either!"

"Suicide bombers?" says Zhu as he slumps into his armchair, briskly tapping an index finger upon its wooden arm. He then quietly exchanges a questioning glance with Cassandra.

"It's not something that we'd do," Cassandra replies to Kali in a soft confident voice. "It sounds more like the kind of thing that Rapture Raiders engineer."

"I got it," says Zhu, sitting up, turning his hand to point a finger at each of them in turn. "You heard that from a governor that it was us, didn't ya? That rat would definitely lump us together as one group to suit his own ends – an' I'm sure he knew it was Raiders of the Rapture too."

The people in the room begin a heavy debate between each other.

He turns to face away again and says, nonchalantly, "So... I ask you... again! What were you doing here when your friend was taken? Something for the governors?"

"It seems like you definitely can't leave here then," smirks the woman. "You naughty children and you thought we'd hel–"

"There is no fooling us," interrupts Zhu with an authoritative voice. "Y' lot are under arrest of the Neos."

"You can't!" Charini cries. "People are sick where we live! They're depending upon us!"

Instant dread comes to Charini, with this moment in time vividly appearing as the fork in the road that leads to guaranteed failure. No more Sangha. No more Bodhi. A gamble taken against the City Centre has failed again, probably just like Bodhi's.

In the background Charini can still hear an argument waging, with Zhu currently serving from his side: "We exist to give the general population a well-needed kick in the arse. Who are you to put your wants above the needs of the many?"

"But we're these people's last chance!" bellows Ash.

"And we're the last chance for everyone!"

Charini suddenly hears a deafening boom and experiences the floor shaking. Everything rattles momentarily as dirt falls from the concrete ceiling. The argument has stopped instantly and everyone is still and silent, on alert for whatever might come next.

"Now what the earth was that?" blurts out Zhu.

Charini hears a muffled yell come from the direction of the stairwell behind her.

"Raiders!"

Zhu slams his hands on the arms of the chair as he stands up.

A head pops in through the stairwell doorway, of a man wearing strange goggles and a metal hat.

"It's a siege! Not government ones, but Rapture ones, only a block away!"

The people there need to hear nothing more. Everyone scrambles; the scene is a mess of scampering bodies.

Another loud boom obscures the sound of all else and the room shakes again.

Charini feels Ash grab her hand and proceed to pull her in a lurch towards a side door. As she is led away, she immediately scans the room in search of Kali. Her last glimpse of the teenager is of her sliding her reclaimed naginata onto her back, as she dashes for the stairwell door.

4. MY OPPOSITION?

Kali rounds the first corner of the staircase. The similar steps passing below her become surreal and her distracted thoughts are transported somewhere very familiar: her recurring dream.

The doorway to the first floor suddenly looms. *Rrrgh, I must stay alert!* There is no time for reminiscing here.

She considers whether smashing one of the building's windows with her naginata would draw instant attention; however she finds the floor not only devoid of desks, but window panes too. As she sprints, wind forced to howl between city skyscrapers makes her hair and cloak billow behind her, and it only becomes stronger as she reaches the place where floor-to-ceiling glass once stood.

She kneels, immediately scanning the road and the building's open-air entrance plaza below. Four Rapture Raiders are already in combat with five Neos; three more have run out from an alley across the road, as two more Neos emerge from the main entrance below her.

She pauses in heightened anticipation of what is to come. Considering she knows there are more in the Army than this, she allows herself to be slightly more rested, waiting.

The Raiders of the Rapture appear to her like they all come from differing backgrounds, from young teenage boys to old dispossessed men. But to her there is something they all hold in common; they are fighting like madmen.

Kali brings herself low to lie flat on the cold concrete. She hears crashing noises of others clambering up the stairwell but doesn't turn to look – they are likely heading to higher floors with projectile weapons.

Then she spots him. Across the road, adjacent to the alley, is a derelict bar with a first floor balcony. Lucius himself has appeared and places his hands upon the banister of the balcony, as more Rapture Raiders begin spewing forth from the alleyway. In a loud shout to the tumult below, he declares, "We have come to purge you from holy grounds devoid of your crimes. Leave now!"

Kali grits her teeth. *Whack dumb fools!*

What a warped view of reality. They must be trying really hard to avoid some kind of messed-up internal pain... Maybe being so disconnected is the cause though...

A hurtful chord then strikes her heart of a past event. *Who are really the ones fearing and fighting reality now, eh?*

She spots two Raiders appearing from another alley, down the road to her right, and scrambles across the floor to the side of the octagonal building to observe them.

Rrrgh. What an absolute waste of time. Why are people fighting so hard against each other over ideals?

At that moment, Kali has turned to look back at Lucius, who appears to slam a fist upon the railing of the balcony.

There are those though, who cannot be reasoned with on a rational basis...

...and need even more kind efforts?

All these notions suddenly make her check herself. *Huh, sounds like things someone I know might say...*

It suddenly dawns on her. With the help of the Neo Liberation Army, this may be the chance their small team needed.

So it seems they've left me with no choice...

Whilst watching intently below, she slowly pulls her naginata from the straps on her back.

...as they have Bodhi.

She continues watching the two nearby Rapture Raiders, as they reach the near side of the road and insecurely step closer, each furtively looking for their entrance to the foray. Kali instinctively examines the ground floor below. *It will be swift and unexpected.*

She stops.

Kali normally throws herself immediately into direct action for a cause.

But this is different.

There is something personal. Again. I don't... want... this deeply unsettling feeling...

She can sense that this is also one of those moments that can lead to outcomes that directly affect her future. *Others I know too...*

Kali shakes slightly.

I am not going to let this wash over me! It is time to take a stand!

She then realises that her knuckles are white from the tight grip she has on her staff. Her blood pressure races high.

Kali allows the build-up within her to dissipate, to finally enter that zone where her mind is in a fluid state of observation and response.

The face of only one person enters her mind.

I'm coming for you...

Then she leaps. Bounding from the window ledge, her right foot meets the wall of the adjacent building, only to relaunch herself sideways again. Her other foot meets a column of their building in the same fashion, and she springs off it again to land on the concrete ground.

Kali brings down the blade of her naginata to immediately slash one of the two surprised Rapture Raiders in the hand. The man shrieks in pain and drops the bat he holds, as his teenage accomplice yelps in surprise. He has already lost his chance though; in one continuous motion, Kali swings the wooden end of the staff to then drive it bluntly into his solar plexus.

She shoves the man to the ground and has already scanned the less-crowded zone ahead of her; two more approaching, fifty metres away.

To her left, she spots Zhu and Cassandra. They are crouched behind a burnt-out old car on the kerbside and their hands are wildly gesturing to people on the second floor behind them to bombard an area nearby. Just then, Cassandra turns to her right and slows when she spots Kali. They lock gazes. It seems to Kali like they are both attempting to deduce each other's mindset from afar.

A deafening explosion blasts people near the car. Cassandra nods to Kali and then breaks from their mutual gaze to dash around it and join the fray. Kali chooses that moment to rush forwards too, quickly reaching the other side of the road not far from the alleyway. The man she encounters is already shell-shocked from the explosion and easily dispatched with a blunt knock to the head.

Suddenly a recognisable shape sprints past her; it is Ash, and his form disappears immediately, deep into the struggle.

I... could die here... Kali suddenly realises she potentially stares death in the face. Despite the training, she has never been in a battle of this size before.

But... they have Bodhi!

Two men surprise her simultaneously...

Like a spectator, her mind glimpses Bodhi and herself as they were outside Coop's.

...she violently swings the naginata at the men....

There is no breaking from Bodhi's embrace this time.

...the staff's blade threateningly indicates the border the men will not be crossing...

A version of Bodhi's voice reverberates as he says to her: "I... love... you..."

"Haaaiiiii-arrrrrraaaaaaaagghh!"

Her scream shocks the men, as she throws herself forwards.

I kept telling myself I had nothing to live for, so if I put all my strength into saving Bodhi... I may win everything at the risk of losing nothing.

Her state of mind, her thoughts, her movements, her reactions – everything flows in complete sync, like a dance, her mind seeming to her like an observing third party.

The two men have no chance in her current state. One holds a hand to a gash in his spleen, whilst the other recoils in shock, running and falling backwards to escape to a safer place.

Kali then lowers her naginata, as her mind suddenly halts in disbelief. Momentarily she has spotted a teenager jogging past the end of the alleyway, and she has to recollect herself from her surprise as he pauses in mid-step. With recollection comes comprehension, and she already detects the tingling of the burst of elation that is about to rock her psyche.

He cocks his head as if considering what he might also have seen.

Her heart leaps as she screams out his name. "Bodhi!!"

As he finally begins to slowly shift his weight to face her, carrying a light axe not meant for trees, she gets the creeping suspicion that this scene is odd, like something is amiss. His expression is exposed to be one of extreme fear that slowly contorts to a picture of freaked violence. As he launches himself in her direction, she notices his chest – a dripping bright white cross has been painted across his heavily dirt-stained white tank top.

The metres between them close instantly, and only Kali's instinct wakes her up to block an attempted blow from his axe.

"WHAT?!" she yelps. She forces the axe up with the end of her blade and searches the eyes of the boy she cares for dearly. The whites of his eyes match his wild fast movement, as he lifts the axe again and rushes forwards with a scream.

She blocks immediately with her long staff. "Bodhi! You can't!"

He swings again and again, grunting aggressively and excessively as she blocks each feverish attack.

"No! This isn't you!" she shrieks.

He apparently hears nothing. The force causes her metal staff to shudder and the transmitted rhythm shakes every bone in her body.

For him to be able to do this, she already knows she has allowed him to approach too close.

"Get back!" she cries. "Get back!" she whimpers.

She blocks another of his downward swings with the base of her naginata and, continuing the swing in a spin, instinctively raises the blade end. They are so close to each other that she can feel the breath from his panting, and so she lowers the blade, cowering backwards.

Kali despairingly recognises that her anguish is dragging her inescapably towards faltering. She has already given so much of herself over to this boy, and never contemplated reserving something for turning back. She can only stare fixedly into his eyes as he raises his arms aloft once again, his axe held high.

Then suddenly, like a freight train passing from her right, Bodhi is knocked completely out of her vision by a person wearing a black hood.

A hood with bright yellow edges.

She can only stumble backwards in disoriented shock. Another flurry of a billowed Rural Tribe cloak appears and Ash has also sprinted past her, helping Yazuka to pin Bodhi to the ground.

Deliriously looking about her, panting heavily, Kali finds most of the battlefield already empty; the surviving Rapture Raiders must have fled, whilst people can be seen aiding the injured or searching amongst the dead.

With the full weight of both Ash and now also Yazuka upon him, she hears Bodhi continuing to shriek as he writhes in his attempts to break free.

"Do you think this is clever, huh?!" Ash is barking at Bodhi like he is a child. "What the Dharma do you think you are doing?!"

Dazed and taking another step back, Kali hears the sounds of running footsteps and turns to collide with Charini, who clasps her elbow tightly. Kali doesn't have to drop her eyes much lower to know that Charini is twisting past her, her whole body fixated on watching the two holding down Bodhi.

"Thank you so much Yazuka," she hears Charini manage to croak out amidst her weeping.

Kali doesn't shrug her off, nor move at all.

5. BENEFIT OF THE DOUBT

Charini and the others are seated on the concrete floor of a small empty office of the skyscraper the Army resides in. Bodhi is asleep on his side, also on the floor between them all, with his breathing coming fast and uneven.

It is no natural sleep. Whilst Bodhi had been held down by Yazuka and Ash, Dr Z had arrived on the scene. From what Charini remembers, the doctor had prepared and jabbed Bodhi with a syringe filled with a strange liquid, and Bodhi had passed out instantly. Since then the drug has worn off, but the doctor still keeps Bodhi in a deep sleep using a sedation device placed adjacent to his head.

Yazuka...

She still remembers her awkwardness in talking to him, whilst Ash and Dr Z had carried Bodhi inside quickly.

"How did?" were the first words that had popped out of her mouth.

"Guess concern got the better of me. Headed off in the direction you'd all planned, an' after you left the Wi-Fi zone t'was still pretty easy to eventually pick up Kali's mobile hopelessly blasting connection signals to faraway towers."

"Oh." It kind of made sense to her. "Oh, and thank you so much again Yazuka."

By the way he then avoided her gaze, she had wondered if he was used to getting compliments. It then started to nag her though, that she really should be running after Bodhi, to make sure he was going to be okay. She had found it hard to focus.

"Well... guess should be going now anyway," mumbled Yazuka.

"Really? Do you have to go? You just got here..."

"It looks like it's over here, and... probably should get back to my family," he said as he rubbed the back of his head.

"Oh."

"Anyway, you've found Bodhi now... You've got Ash..."

"Er. Okay..."

"Well... seeya," and with that simple parting remark, Yazuka was gone.

She still remembers blankly watching him walk off, before steeling herself to sprint inside after the others.

Stupid jerk.

Her unhappy cloud has now left her entirely. Seeing Bodhi returned was also a dream, but now she feels she is her real self again, back in her real skin. The events between losing Bodhi and the battle have been a distant whirl, but now she feels a participant once more of each passing moment.

"Good evening everyone," says Dr Z interrupting her thoughts, as he leans through the door of the office.

He motions for them to follow him out of the room. As the last person exits, he closes the door behind him and removes his fisherman's hat to reveal his grey balding head. Charini can't see the equipment bag he normally carries at all.

"Now then. Your friend has unfortunately been put through something the Rapture Raiders have been using on some unfortunate people. By the way he's been attacking you, it's an easy guess that he's another victim of a memory repressor."

"Memory repressor?" Charini racks her brains but hasn't heard of such a thing before.

"It selects a person's unhappy memory, links all the others with it and then amplifies that memory to repress everything."

"Woah," says Ash. "Huh?"

"You see, a person's mental state can stop them from balancing right from wrong. Even when they're good at heart. More-so, and a convenient side-affect for people using this device is, due to the way it works, what the victim treasures most is therefore what they become most averse to."

"Those bastards!" Ash exclaims.

"Unfortunately, even with help, in a similar way to retrograde amnesia... I'm sorry to tell you this, but... large quantities of his memory will never be able to be recovered."

"Never?" squeaks Charini. An image of the Bodhi she knows comes front-and-centre to her mind. Kind Bodhi; the boy she's always known. In her anxiety she turns to consult the quiet Kali, but Kali just seems to be staring at the floor. *I can't comprehend what a life without Bodhi being around will be like... He's always been there...*

"There is a chance. With restoration he may retain some of his memories in dreams. I'm doubtful of anything during his waking hours though."

"Are you saying he's permanently in this messed-up state?" asks Ash, who's suddenly sounding to Charini like a freaked-out parent.

"Well, if we can release the memory that is forcing down all the others, it might help him to relax considerably."

"So how are you going to do this? Let's do it!"

"Hypnotherapy," Dr Z replies to him in a strong reassuring voice.

Ash nods, but then stops like he doesn't quite get it. "And this is going to work?"

"It could be messy... You all – his antagonists – will have to stay out of sight until he is fully under hypnosis. Once he is, then I will need all of you to help the boy... in battling himself."

It is quiet. Charini focuses on the doctor and, without checking, she is sure that everyone else is too.

"Okay?"

They all nod in unison, and Dr Z allows only himself to slip into the room with Bodhi.

Charini and Ash cast serious questioning glances at each other.

"You don't think Bodhes is permanently in this state, do you?"

"I'm sure the doc will do his best," says Ash, but Charini doesn't find this assuring. *Only hours ago, Bodhi was Kali's opponent...*

They are suddenly interrupted by a scream: "Who the Dharma are you?!"

It is pretty obvious to Charini that the sedative device has just been removed from Bodhi's head.

From then on she can only hear muffled voices from the room. Bodhi's distressing incredulous voice is easy to identify. After numerous exchanges, the voices slowly die down until, eventually, there is silence.

"I'm going in," says Ash.

Charini is about to tell him that he's not supposed to, when the door opens slightly to reveal the doctor's face. Wordlessly, he motions for them to enter.

They slowly step into the abnormally silent room. She expected to find Bodhi raving mad and tied up in a corner, but instead discovers him to be still lying on the concrete floor, flat on his back with his hands folded neatly across his chest.

"How did you even get this far?" whispers Ash.

The doctor also responds in a whisper. "Well, hypnotic suggestion cannot work at all unless the person has a desire to go along with it."

"How on earth did you get that?"

"I told him what I was going to do. When he questioned how he could trust my so-called repaired memories being true, I said it was his choice. But, and I reminded him..." the doctor glances at the others resuming their places surrounding Bodhi. "In the Rapture Raiders' truth... he was a slave."

He turns from Ash and they both join the group.

"Bodhi, I need you to tell us something," the Doctor announces in a confident voice. "It is something that should be constantly on your mind. Something that is worrying you a lot, even right now."

"Garyo!" snaps Bodhi instantly, sitting up and awake in anger, which shocks everyone around him. Except for Dr Z., that is. Bodhi's raspy voice dissipates into a creaking whimper of woe, his eyes slowly returning to closed again.

Realisation has immediately settled on Charini. *Garyo Bensen.* She recognises the name, for it brings forth sadness from her early childhood, images of a boy leering at her from a tree. *The boy who constantly teased me for having no dad... I eventually got over it, but maybe Bodhi–*

"Garyo said..." creaks Bodhi.

"You're in a safe place Bodhi," croons Dr Z.

Garyo beat on so many of us... what a poor disturbed boy he was then...

"He's so unreasonable?!" spat Bodhi. "Stupid plans and ideas! How could we even agree on anything, let alone live under the same roof!"

That was him alright...

Bodhi is so panicky, speaking so much faster than normal, that Charini can't tell where Bodhi's unhappy memory ends and his memory-repressed affliction begins. *He's not even his pondering self... have we really lost him?*

"Garyo said... I would never amount to anything... that people would be out of their minds to like a guy like me..."

Charini feels she has to say something and, by the doctor's continuing silence, assumes it must be part of the plan.

"Bodhi, it's not true, you are surrounded by people that love you right now."

Dr Z nods to her.

"Yeah matey," chimes in Ash. "Me too, and there are plenty more at home who do as well."

Bodhi is silent, his inner workings unfathomable to Charini.

She then realises Kali hasn't added anything. Charini looks to her, and finds the girl's vision to be fixated on Bodhi, her body rigid.

She nudges her. "Kali?"

Kali frowns menacingly at her for an instant, but the girl's worried attention is immediately back on Bodhi.

"I..." Kali drops her mouth open momentarily, but closes it again. Her eyes dart furiously to her shoulder, as she leans and hunches her shoulders forwards.

C'mon Kali....

"Heyyy Bodhi-man," jumps in Ash instead. "If you remember that boy, then don't you remember what the Sangha teaches about bullies too? Huh?" he says slowly. "For one thing, hey, they're showing how not to be... they're oppressed by ways that find it hard to get to overall better outcomes. Yeah?"

"Yeah," Charini quietly recalls.

"But he's against me!" Bodhi's voice desperately rings out, his eyes still closed.

Thoughts of Tylanni are also entering Charini's mind, the history between them, and the now. These feelings well up inside her.

"Don't forget, somewhere, this boy is also hurting."

A prayer for Garyo, Tylanni, Bodhi; for everyone.

"He's doing this to vainly protect his own insecurities... just like you. Despite how poorly, he aims to avoid unhappiness with the tools at hand to him... just like you. There is... just like Alexis said... common ground..."

Bodhi's shoulders suddenly sag and he lets out a huge sigh, receding like a hot air balloon with open vents. Everyone sits back. With his eyes still closed, Bodhi rolls to lie on his side again, seeming that he is ready to fall into a deep sleep.

Charini sees Dr Z turn to face them all, and his huge beaming smile means only one thing to her. She experiences a strong surge of excitement, of anticipation.

"Okay now," he says to them all. "Just remember to treat him as you normally would, despite his loss. Familiarity will make things easier for him."

The doctor turns back to Bodhi. "Bodhi, you are still in that safe place, and are very lucky to have such sincere friends. After three I will click my fingers, and you will wake. One... two... three..."

Bodhi groggily opens his eyes to a furore of friends calling to him, Charini included. "Bodhi! Bodhes!"

"Okay, okay everyone," says the doctor. "One at a time."

Charini sees Dr Z indicate with his open palm to the first person on his left, which happens to be a startled Kali. She swallows and moves forwards on her knees slightly.

To Charini, Bodhi looks far more relaxed than before. Even the expression on his face is familiar to her again.

"Uh... it's good... that you're... okay..." Kali says to Bodhi half nonchalantly, him still sitting up but now with a gaping mouth.

There is a moment of silence, which feels uncomfortable. Bodhi then looks to the others, and in the silence he must have realised they all expect a response.

He stares back into Kali's now searching eyes. "I... I'm..." he stutters.

Charini waits with baited breath. *Please. Be you again...*

"I'm really sorry but... I... can't recall who you are..."

Charini sees Kali's eyes visibly droop, as she feels her own heart dive.

"I have flashes of... familiar feelings... but everything is so... fleeting..."

"It's okay," Kali says slowly, but then her gaze partially rises. "This time around," she says feebly, swallowing again. "You can... depend on me..."

6. THE FIRST STEP IN A JOURNEY

Only minutes after Bodhi had been released from his mental prison, a tall woman with red hair strode into the room. How this person related to the group of strangers around him was a mystery, but the other three seemed to know her, as the conversation went mute immediately.

"So I see you've all found your friend," she had said to nobody in particular, but her hazel-coloured stern eyes focused upon him. "Good evening young man, my name's Cassandra," was all she said.

Everyone remained silent, so Bodhi did the same. Whilst only feeling like he had met this girl named Charini in the past few minutes, Bodhi thought he could tell that she was feeling uneasy.

"Looks like everyone has come out okay," said the woman as she surveyed the room. "That's good. We try to keep ourselves well hidden, so they likely misjudged us."

Everyone there nodded.

"Hmmm. So. About our earlier conversation," and Bodhi saw that she had her entire attention on Charini.

Crud. Earlier? I already have no idea what this woman is talking about. He could definitely sense the tension in the room though.

"So... tell me... what were you all doing for the governors?"

"Oh, in exchange... for a cure for our people..." Bodhi saw that Charini was looking to her companions, seeming unsure about what to say. The girl named Kali was signalling her with a strange frown, and odd incomprehensible expressions were on the face of the guy named Ash. Bodhi himself was dying to know, as he didn't have a clue.

"Don't be afraid," said Cassandra. "We're on the side of the people, like you. Not the governors."

"Uh... the governor... wanted us to find... you."

Bodhi heard Kali groan.

The room fell silent as an expressionless Cassandra stared at Charini. The tension he felt in the room became enormous.

Then Cassandra suddenly burst out in a mix of raucous laughter and giggles, gripping her sides like she had been holding it in all along. The others in the room appeared shocked.

The woman eventually calmed down.

"That's all?" She wiped a tear from her eye. "Maybe we can work together then."

"Er, I don't quite understand," said Charini. Neither did Bodhi.

"Give our location to the governor."

"What?" Kali blurted out.

"Zhu will take some convincing, and I don't think he'll completely agree with me," said Cassandra as she cocked her head to brush some of her long red hair past her shoulder. "There'll be no choice though once you're let go," she said with a wicked smile. "But, it's to save your tribe – it's a worthy cause."

"But won't that cause huge problems for you?" asked Charini incredulously.

Cassandra held a bemused smirk as she chuckled again deep in her throat. "Don't worry about us. We'll move on soon enough, whilst still ensuring there's enough evidence left to be seen from the air. We always have to move, eventually."

The faces in the room had seemed expectantly happy, carefully consulting with each other without uttering a word.

"Think about it, it makes a governor help a Rural Tribe, something that sounds fun to me."

"Thank you so much Cassandra!" had cried Charini finally. Bodhi saw her smack her knees like she really wanted to get up and hug the woman, but she held herself back.

"Hah! Where's Zhu so we can thank him too?" said the young man named Ash.

"I'd probably hold off on that," said Cassandra with a little laugh. "The result will be enough for him."

Bodhi felt that from then on the whirlwind of events never stopped for him. So much was occurring and he was okay if people sometimes forgot to explain to him what exactly was transpiring. With little knowledge to dwell on the past or future, Bodhi was acutely aware of the passing of time and events in the present. Their group had eventually left the dead city by foot, only to come to enter another city that was so bustling that it made Bodhi feel claustrophobic.

So much to remember, so much excitement around him. He had felt that sometimes he should fake it a bit and join in, to be included, and also just because everyone was so happy.

Thinking of the people he is dependent on brings him back to the present. Bodhi is loitering about, with Kali and Charini, on a quiet street of what he has been told is called the Outer Rim. The squat plain buildings all look similar to him. Apparently it is a government administration area. None of them have much to do as they wait. Kali is currently leaning against one of the buildings, whilst Charini sits on the concrete path, also with her back to the wall.

These people are still around him, even now, and he is thankful for that. Bodhi can't exactly remember much about these people, but his gut feelings tell him he has shared many experiences with them. *I think my gut is going to be relied upon a lot... for a while anyway...*

They have not much longer to wait until finally Bodhi sees Ash come out from the building across the street, the thin metal door swinging open to hit the side wall with a loud bang. He is carrying a large crate full of small brown plastic bottles. Everyone except for Bodhi seems to have an investment in the occasion, since they expectantly hurry over to Ash as he crashes the crate onto the sidewalk.

"So it went well?" he hears Charini's small voice pounce eagerly, as Kali and Bodhi approach them slowly from behind. Bodhi notices Kali is quiet, but her eyes are open wide.

Ash mentions something about a governor and aerial reconnaissance drones, which sounds pretty exciting to Bodhi. He wants to ask more but doesn't feel like interrupting for an explanation; he has been doing so a lot lately.

Charini and Ash have already started unpacking the crate and stuffing the bottles of liquid into backpacks belonging to all of them.

"We can finally go home!" Charini cries aloud. She pauses in the middle of packing the bottles, and begins to weep uncontrollably. Bodhi isn't worried though. Anybody can tell that they are tears of letting go, of happiness.

She looks up and he is caught out watching her. She then gives him such a beaming teary smile that he cannot help but give her a smile in return. It feels like something unsaid between them, that gives him the impression of a long history of connection between them both, despite no recollection at all.

"Ha, a Rural Tribe saved by the king of City Raiders, woulda never believed it!" quips Ash.

Charini continues wearily sobbing as she starts packing again, but appears to be okay.

Kali is still watching from the rear of the group. She folds her arms and throws a dirty look to the back of Ash's head.

Humph, whatever.

She leans her back against a wall again and flips open her smartphone, wanting to remove herself from the flowing emotions.

Kali hasn't gone online in ages, and there are hundreds of notifications from her differing accounts on the Internet.

Too much... She begins logging into each account and deleting them.

Hearing Charini's cry about home has left that word lingering throughout her mind. She starts to consider what random things might be in her future, but she knows she's wasting her time.

She knows that she's already decided.

On second thoughts... She edges over to a public waste bin and checks around. Once the coast is clear, she surreptitiously places her hand inside and lets the phone slip from her hand, unnoticed.

~

High-rises unto small single-storey dwellings unto hardly any buildings at all. They reach the outskirts of the Outer Rim and their surroundings mainly entail farmland, old roads and many power-lines. Some houses appear to Charini like they were previously barns and she assumes much farmland has been abandoned and reused.

Many old vehicles laden with foodstuffs speed past them as they maintain a slow walking pace beside the road. She observes that Kali has automatically taken the lead, and chuckles to herself briefly, but then realises that she herself has fallen into step beside Ash. Charini knows Bodhi is trailing behind them, but not too far for her to worry.

With each recognisable difference in scenery, Charini's excitement grows further, but something seems missing, giving her a nagging feeling of emptiness.

At least an hour passes, and their slow walk becomes a trance of similar repeating scenery.

She gazes dreamily at the heavily worked land over the adjacent wire fence. The corn plants look slightly brown and thirsty.

Instantly she has a vision of the endless rows of the food-bearing orchards of the Sangha; Nima chuckling as Tylanni drops the fruit she has picked; Bodhi's mum holding a woven basket to her side and smiling in the sun; the food being shared out around the evening fire amongst laughter and happiness.

Her daydream of bountiful crops, the land, the sun – it begins to extend from the Sangha and back towards them, following paths they are soon to travel. She isn't concerned with having to walk so far – it is the potential for ecosystems that populate her mind, driven by the sun and water, which continue running even when the moon and stars come out at night. She feels small, dwarfed by these.

When I was in the Rim, being around so many people for so long makes you feel that all that is important is people; people's events, people's problems, people's achievements... taking a step outside it though...

The sheer relative enormous scale of the ecosystems reaching about the world re-enters her mind. She is such a tiny part of it all. This smallness relaxes her immensely.

However, that's not it; the missing feeling is still there.

She decides to disregard it for now.

Charini knows her journey has made her a different person. Her dreams for everyone on earth to be good to the environment, and leading easier happier healthy lives... *How arrogant. How I wished everyone would become like Rural Tribes...*

The group has been silent for a while and, speaking to nobody in particular, Charini feels she has to speak her mind. "As Rural Tribes we're trying, but we also have our own flaws, just as the city does. I mean, the Outer Rim is not a failed attempt at emulating us – being as 'new age' and 'modern' as us – they have their own beliefs and views of the world... what it means to be alive... don't you think?"

"Ha, well I..." Ash begins. "That's a whole bunch of stuff there. I don't know..."

The confused response from him makes her sheepishly realise that her head really is just a muddle of thoughts, and not the consistent revelation she had thought it to be.

Charini hears a voice behind her.

"If some of us feel... confident enough... to start for... something new..."

She looks over her shoulder to find Bodhi still partially deep in thought. *That sounds like the Bodhi I know.*

She sees Kali twist around, the girl's eyes seeking her out. They exchange knowing glances, and she notices Kali has a slight smile at the corner of her mouth. Charini starts to get the feeling that Kali is quite a lot more relaxed than her usual self.

Not receiving much more than Bodhi's response though, Charini returns to mulling and reminiscing. *Nomads are quite different to us too, like the one Bodhi said he saw recently...* She has no personal recollection of the man, but continues daydreaming as they walk regardless.

She envisions a group of six nomadic families crossing a rocky desert by foot. They carry hardly any possessions about them at all. For a moment Charini imagines one of them painstakingly dragging along Yazuka's TV window, and giggles to herself.

By evening the nomads have come to rest by a campfire amongst a treed oasis. Bodhi's old man is there, and he is telling a story to earnestly listening children. As he finishes it with a smile, they all laugh at his punch line. Everyone in the camp is relaxed and the laughter is infectious.

Bodhi had said he encountered the man by the Sangha's fire one night...

A strange old man, he relaxes quietly alone by the crackling Sangha fire. A black-and-white striped cloth, common to nomads, is draped across his head to his shoulders, and his skin is weathered from a dry desert life.

Oh, Kali was probably there too...

The image of the man by the fire now includes both Kali and Bodhi, conferring about the old man, their quiet whispers drawing each other closer–

Humph.

I'll be home soon. Yes, that's what's important!

Charini raises a palm to the air and announces, "Goodbye Outer Rim... and not long from now, hello home!"

She stops walking mid-pace.

"...home is where the heart is..."

It is something that she heard from Grandpa, what feels like ages ago.

"I..."

Despite so much being resolved, she knows that empty spot is not going away, what has been left unsaid. Maybe something she also misunderstood?

She hears the others eventually stop and, despite her staring at the ground, she knows they've all turned to face her.

"Need a rest Chaz?" questions Ash. "These packs are all heavy now, and a few minutes rest every now and then won't be a total disaster."

"After this far?" complains Kali, feigning pain.

A rest is not really what she has been thinking of, but it is welcome nonetheless. *Once all this is over and done, I hope Yazuka and his family will be okay if I come and visit sometime...*

Bodhi's busy mind is still meandering around what Charini has recently mentioned. Her words have been like a light, shining on topics that spark in his mind.

"Their own beliefs and views of the world."

Everything is strange to Bodhi lately, including the people travelling with him.

He looks over to where Kali is. She is leaning forwards with her elbows atop the fence, gazing far off past the fields to where they themselves are soon to be headed. It's the first time he's seen her silky black hair without a ponytail, and long hanging strands dance in the slight breeze.

Apparently I know her, but...

"Just what do you think you're looking at, huh?"

Crud. "It's... not like... uh, I, I meant anything by it," he stammers.

"And it's not like I'm coming to the Sangha for you, either!"

He notices Ash has a big grin on his face, and so Bodhi retorts "Ha... sure."

Kali's mouth gapes in surprise as she then swings her whole body fast to face away from him, and her long hair swirls. "Humph, pervert!"

Bodhi is flustered. *Dammit... now what does this odd girl think?* His mind calms fast though.

He avoids turning to face her again too, but rekindles his last image of her in his mind's eye.

She sure seems to know me... and seems to have confidence in me like these other people show....

I hardly know anything about her though... but...

...

Despite the fire inside...

This girl...

She does... look cute...

Then suddenly, without warning, tears.

Silent tears are rolling down his cheeks.

I... don't... understand... ?

His whole heart then surges like it is shouting at him, like something incredibly important is amiss, but it just won't come to him. As he was told – irretrievably lost.

Momentarily he is angry with himself for his constant lack of comprehension, but anger at something unknown can only last for so long.

He reminds himself as the doctor has told him – that unexpected things may happen often, and that some things, in a way, they may be reclaimed, given time.

AUTHOR'S NOTE

First and foremost, many thanks goes to Ben Rowley and Erin O'Donnell for reviewing some of the earlier prototypes. Without you I couldn't have improved the work. Special thanks also goes to my wife for putting up with, or getting used to, me occasionally disappearing into this world of words.

I was riding a train one day, holding my bike, musing on the way to work. I had no intention of writing a novel, though we don't always plan these things.

It had been less than a year since governments of the world had met together on Climate Change in Copenhagen: an ambitious meet up that, despite the hopes of the world, provided no concrete result. Reflecting on it once more, somehow my wandering mind led me to fictional futures, and eventually Rural Tribes and City Raiders. The moment I could get near something to write with, I noted everything down.

I also love fiction with a very prominent mix of philosophy and teenage adventure. There are some very good authors out there, however I wish for more stories than I've found so far!

So, you see, I had no choice – ha. After numerous casual nights of spare time, it was nice to complete the main body of text on Christmas night of 2012.

I hope you've enjoyed reading this tale as much as I've enjoyed writing and sharing it with you.

Best Regards,

G. C. Huxley

http://www.huxley.id.au